THE DATING PROPOSAL

LAUREN BLAKELY

COPYRIGHT

ALSO BY LAUREN BLAKELY

Big Rock Series

Big Rock

Mister O

Well Hung

Full Package

Joy Ride

Hard Wood

One Love Series

The Sexy One

The Only One

The Hot One

The Knocked Up Plan

Come As You Are

The Heartbreakers Series

Once Upon a Real Good Time

Once Upon a Sure Thing

Once Upon a Wild Fling

Sports Romance

Most Valuable Playboy

Most Likely to Score

Lucky In Love Series

Best Laid Plans

The Feel Good Factor

Nobody Does It Better

Always Satisfied Series

Satisfaction Guaranteed (June 2019)

Instant Gratification (September 2019)

Standalone

Stud Finder

The V Card

Wanderlust

Part-Time Lover

The Real Deal

Unbreak My Heart

The Break-Up Album

21 Stolen Kisses

Out of Bounds

Unzipped

Birthday Suit

The Dating Proposal (May 2019)

Never Have I Ever (Fall 2019)

The Caught Up in Love Series

Caught Up In Us

Pretending He's Mine

Playing With Her Heart

Stars In Their Eyes Duet

My Charming Rival

My Sexy Rival

The No Regrets Series

The Thrill of It

The Start of Us

Every Second With You

The Seductive Nights Series

First Night (Julia and Clay, prequel novella)

Night After Night (Julia and Clay, book one)

After This Night (Julia and Clay, book two)

One More Night (Julia and Clay, book three)

A Wildly Seductive Night (Julia and Clay novella, book 3.5)

The Joy Delivered Duet

Nights With Him (A standalone novel about Michelle and Jack)

Forbidden Nights (A standalone novel about Nate and Casey)

The Sinful Nights Series

Sweet Sinful Nights

Sinful Desire

Sinful Longing

Sinful Love

The Fighting Fire Series

Burn For Me (Smith and Jamie)

Melt for Him (Megan and Becker)

Consumed By You (Travis and Cara)

The Jewel Series

A two-book sexy contemporary romance series

The Sapphire Affair

The Sapphire Heist

ABOUT

One woman on a dating quest. One man in need of a relationship guru.
   One wild proposal neither can resist.

Watch out world -- I'm ready to date again.

The seven years I invested in my ex left me with nothing but scorch marks from the way he peeled out and left me at the altar. I'm not looking to put my heart into a relationship any time soon.

What I *am* looking for? To have some freaking fun. My best friends can't wait to set me up with suitable single guys, and soon I've got three promising prospects. Then I bump into Chris....

Clever and funny, with a sexy surfer's bod and a brilliant nerd brain, he has just the right screwdriver to fix my hard drive. (Yes, the one for my computer.)

I wouldn't mind dating him. The trouble is he just proposed to me—to be the new dating guru on his TV show—and I said yes.

***

Don't get your honey where you get your money.

I'd make a sign or put that mantra on a tattoo, except I'm not likely to forget it, given that the last time I mixed business with pleasure, it almost tanked my career. Now? I play by the book.

That hasn't been a problem until McKenna. She's engaging and fun, quick with a snapback or a sensitive, sensible reply—perfect for my TV show. Too bad she's also perfectly kissable.

But I lock my feelings down. We've both worked too hard on our careers to let our connection go further than some sexy banter...and, okay, one impulsive, fantastic kiss—no matter how much our boss, our fans, and our friends propose we make our on-screen chemistry an off-screen romance.

What happens when you meet the right person at the wrong time?

Note: Back in the day, I wrote a book called TROPHY HUSBAND, and though it's no longer available for sale, the characters of Chris and McKenna seemed to demand another chance in the spotlight. THE DATING PROPOSAL is a complete reimagining of their romance, with 85 percent brand-new material, a fresh plot, and vastly expanded characterizations so you can come to know and love Chris and McKenna like I do. Enjoy!

AUTHOR'S NOTE

Dear Reader,

Back in the day, I wrote a book called TROPHY HUSBAND, and though it's no longer available for sale, the characters of Chris and McKenna seemed to demand another chance in the spotlight. THE DATING PROPOSAL is a complete reimagining of their romance, with 85 percent brand-new material, a fresh plot, and vastly expanded characterizations so you can come to know and love Chris and McKenna like I do. Enjoy!

xoxo
    Lauren

1

MCKENNA

Today is my anniversary, and I plan to celebrate in style.

I slide into my favorite skinny jeans, grab my lucky Michael Kors bag, and cinch on a slim rose-gold bracelet my sister gave me.

Boom. I twirl in front of my roommate. "Everything look good?"

Ms. Pac-Man raises her snout from her dog bed, one of many in her collection.

"Can I take that as a fashion hound sign of approval?"

She wags her fluffy yellow flag of a tail.

"Excellent. I thought you'd agree." I bend and give her a kiss on the nose, and she places a big paw on my leg. "Yes, I love you too."

And I'm off to a solo Monday breakfast that happens to mark a special occasion.

I head downstairs to the garage, into the car, and onto the street, driving past a local organic grocery store, a hipster cafe, and a cake shop I believe uses alchemical powers in its batter. One evening many months ago when I was feeling particularly blue, I stumbled in and tried to erase my sorrows with a marble chocolate cake that I was sure would cure my broken heart with its magical elixirs. Alas, the owner handed me a napkin, told me *there, there*, and said my tears had probably ruined the slice, so I should try another tomorrow when she baked a new cake. On the house.

You bet your ass I went there the next day for my free sympathy slice. Admittedly, I felt a bit better. Go, cake.

Today, I'm not crying in my dessert. No chance. No way.

I'm officially done mourning the death of my almost-marriage.

As I drive, I turn the radio up louder. I sing along to the music—Frank Sinatra's "I've Got You Under My Skin"—as I motor up steep hills then down a roller-coaster dip on my way into Hayes Valley. The station shifts to playing the King, another favorite of this retro music–loving girl, and he's now crooning "Can't Help Falling in Love."

My favorite song ever.

The song Todd didn't want to be our wedding song, since he'd insisted on "Have I Told You Lately"—the perfect tune, since that was how he felt about me, he'd claimed.

And you know what?

I turn it all the way up and sing along like I'm getting paid.

He can't get me down anymore.

I love this song. It's mine. It belongs to me and only me now.

A red Honda scoots out of the prime spot right in front of a restaurant coolly named Madcap, next to the diner where I'm going. As I glide my orange MINI Cooper into the space, I mouth a silent *thank you* to the parking gods. I happen to have excellent parking karma and my ex has the shittiest, which simply reaffirms my belief in, well, karma.

Then again, it would be awfully hard to have good karma if you're, say, the kind of person who dumps your fiancée via voicemail the day before your wedding.

"Listen, I've had a change of heart. I met someone else, and as much as it pains me to do this the day before, well, hey, better than the day after! What do you say we call the whole thing off?" he'd said in his phone message.

One year later, I'm most decidedly not celebrating the anniversary of our loving union, but I am celebrating this fantastic parking spot. And all things considered, especially given how ridiculously hard it is to find one in this city, I'll take the sliver of space for my auto, thank you very much.

I open the door and snatch my bag from the seat. I consider this purse lucky because the same day I bought it, a new investment group contacted me with an offer. And it can't hurt to have some luck on my side today. When I reach the sidewalk, I catch a glimpse of a familiar figure, a tall, dark-haired man. I don't know his name, but I see him occasionally, and I think he works at Madcap. Every now and then he'll say, "Hey there" or "How's it going?" He's friendly and has excellent taste in clothes. His charcoal slacks and navy-blue button-down look like they came from Barneys. He's chatting on his phone, pacing in front of the restaurant. He looks up, notices me, and shoots me a smile.

It's kind of sweet and sexy at the same time, and I feel a little flurry of, dare I say, butterflies in my belly.

That's interesting. Hmm. I haven't felt those in a long time.

And you know what? I welcome their return. Not with a parade or anything grandiose, but maybe a banner and some glitter, and hey, glitter can be cool.

I give a small smile and head next door to The Best Diner in the City, which I suspect was named for Search Engine Optimization. It also happens to be completely accurate so I come here once a week and have for the last year.

Dining alone doesn't hurt anymore, thanks to this self-assigned therapy. I'm a big believer in hoisting yourself up by your garter belt, so I ate here alone the first weekend after the breakup, and then did it again and again until the aching stopped. Even though I'd found this place a few years ago and came here occasionally, Todd never went with me to this diner. He said he didn't care for cheap, hole-in-the-wall eateries. Fine by me. This diner feels like mine. Gloriously all mine.

The hostess guides me to one of the last remaining two-tops. I sit and run a hand along the slightly distressed fabric of my skinny jeans. Designer brand at a bargain-basement sale. Another of life's little wins.

I order my usual—scrambled eggs and toast, opting for a Diet Coke because it's a celebration. A minute later, the waitress brings me a can and a glass of ice. I thank her then crack it open, indulging in one of my *un-guilty* pleasures as I savor the first effervescent burst and the taste of the cold metal on my lips.

One of the great benefits of dining alone, as I've learned, is there's no one to steal the first sip from me.

How about that for another win?

I pour the rest into the glass then reach for my laptop from my bag.

As I flip open the computer to work on my fashion blog, the waitress guides a gorgeous young redhead over to the table next to me. As if on autopilot, I scan her outfit—sparkling white running shoes with a pink swirly stripe, black workout pants, and a color-coordinated snug workout top—she looks rather peppy.

She flashes a warm smile. "Hi."

"Hey."

"This placed is jammed today. Weird for a Monday."

"It's like this every day. The food is amazing."

"I've heard great things about it. I'm so excited to finally give it a try."

Maybe I won't need the laptop. Perhaps this gal and I will chat for the next thirty minutes, seeing as she's mighty friendly. "You won't be disappointed. Everything's good."

"My husband said he's been wanting to go to this place for the longest time. He's just out parking the car.

We couldn't find a spot nearby." She tips her forehead to the door.

I half expected her to say her dad was going to join her because she looks like a teenager. But maybe she was a teenage bride. "Both of you will love it, then. I'm a regular. A *devotee*, as they say," I add in a British accent, just for fun.

She laughs. "What do you recommend?"

"Anything. Except hard-boiled eggs, because they're gross."

"They're the most disgusting food ever."

I lean closer and say in a conspiratorial whisper, "My ex used to love them. I couldn't even be in the house when he ate hard-boiled eggs."

"You want to hear something funny? My husband used to love them too. But I laid down the law. No hard-boiled eggs ever in my home. I cured him of his hard-boiled egg addiction like that." She snaps her fingers.

I hold up a hand to high-five her. "You deserve major points."

"Oh, look. There he is." When I turn to follow her gaze, it's as if I've had a pair of cleats jammed into my belly. This is what it feels like when the batter slides into home and you're the catcher who's not wearing a chest protector.

The diner shrinks. The walls close in, gripping me. I can't breathe. This has to be a mistake. An error.

Todd's here.

He freezes when he sees me then quickly recovers, taking the seat across from his wife.

The girl-child I've been chatting with, my new

breakfast-best-friend, is the college-age creature from Vegas who won his heart before he said "I do." The woman he met the weekend of his bachelor party.

And you know what?

It doesn't hurt like a pair of cleats any longer.

Sure, I feel a tinge of frustration that I can't continue this chat with her.

A small dose of annoyance that my breakfast is zooming toward unpleasant territory, to say the least.

But the pain? The shock? Just as quickly as they arrived, they exit. Gone, simply gone.

The walls return to normal.

I breathe easily.

"Hi, McKenna," Todd says in his best business-like voice.

"Oh . . ." Amber releases a long, slow breath as her mouth drops open, and she shifts her gaze from him to me, registering who she's been chatting with. "I'm so sorry."

But I'm going to be the bigger person. After all, today is an awesome day. "Nice to meet you, Amber. And congratulations on the hard-boiled egg cure. That is seriously awesome. I'd love to sit here and chat with you, but I have a blog to write and then some business plans to review. But I hope you love everything here. Enjoy!"

"You know, why don't we just get a new table?" Amber says to Todd.

He scans the restaurant. This is the last empty one. "We can leave. We'll find someplace else," he says, and his voice is the definition of contrition. This is the Todd I knew—polite no matter what.

But I'm not letting him have the last word on breakfast. He might have gotten it when it came to marrying me, but he does not get to leave this place too. I put on my best professional smile. "Please stay. I was telling Amber that you haven't lived unless you've eaten here. It's the best."

He glances at her, asking for permission. She lifts her brows, unsure, but I can tell she's bending.

"It's all good, guys," I add, with a smile.

"Okay, then. We shall stay." He reaches for a menu and scans it.

And I conduct a scan of my emotions.

There's no stinging feeling in the back of my eyes. There are no tears I'm keeping at bay. There's . . . *nothing*.

I want to break out in song.

I want to kiss the sky.

I am over him. Over him. *Over him!*

He closes the menu and shoots me the smile that had been part of my life for the better part of a decade. That patented grin that won me over when I first met him. "And how is everything with you?"

"Great," I say, so brightly that it sounds fake, only it's not, because what on the planet could be greater than knowing you're over the weasel you almost married?

The waitress brings me my food. She turns to Todd and Amber. They order as I set to work.

As I eat and type, I beam inside.

This is the start of the next phase in my life.

Lucky bag, indeed.

When I'm through, I pay the bill, pack up my laptop, and say goodbye to Todd, Amber, and the last year of my life.

Hello, world. I'm back.

With a spring in my step, I head to my car, where I see a white piece of paper tucked under the wiper, flapping in the wind.

My step unsprings. A parking ticket? That's not how parking karma works.

I turn around to peer up at the sign. I haven't gone past the two-hour limit. I glance at the curb. It's not red. There's no hydrant nearby. I survey the block, and down near the corner of Hayes Street, the meter man is writing a ticket for a Prius. I grab the slip from my windshield and march toward him. Today is my lucky day, and I'm going to make sure it keeps being awesome.

In my best friendly, problem solver voice, I say, "Hey there! Can we chat about this?"

He turns around to face me, and I point to my car. He looks from it to the paper I'm waving, back to me. "I didn't give you a ticket, lady."

He walks the other way.

"I put that there."

When I spin around, I'm face-to-face with the guy who shops at Barneys.

2

MCKENNA

Up close, he's even better looking. His face is chiseled, his light-blue eyes sparkle, and his brown hair looks amazingly soft. I can't help but give him a quick up and down perusal. It's clear he's completely sculpted underneath those clothes.

"Hey there. I saw you earlier when you parked."

Parked.

Grr. Did I ding his car and not even realize it? I bet he protects that car's paint job like a mama bear. I crane my neck to inspect, but the Lexus in front of my MINI Cooper seems dingless. "Did I hit your car?"

Laughing, he shakes his head. "No. Great parking job, by the way." He flashes a million-dollar smile at me.

Have I slipped into an alternate universe? Hot men don't compliment me on my parking.

I mean, I can park my ass off, but it's not something that usually draws male attention.

"Why, thank you," I say, jutting out a hip, figuring

nice is the way to play off whatever I did to warrant a windshield note. "I've been hoping someone would notice my parallel parking skills."

"Oh, I noticed. And I was duly impressed."

He tips his forehead to the white slip of paper in my hand. "So what do you think?"

I furrow my brow. "Of this?" I hold it up.

"Yeah." His smile is magnetic.

I open it. And it's not a parking summons, nor is it a *bitch, you hit my car*-gram.

It's something odder.

Something I never could have predicted.

"You're gorgeous. Give me a call sometime. I'd love to take you out. The name is Steven Crane. I own Madcap." His number is scribbled at the bottom of the note.

I stand there befuddled, maybe even as far as gobsmacked. "You're asking me out?"

"I've seen you here most weeks. Been trying to get up the nerve to talk to you. Today you seemed to have a spring in your step, and I thought maybe it was a sign to finally go for it. I'm recently divorced, so I'm a little out of practice in the dating world. Hope it's okay I left a note."

"What do you know? I'm totally out of practice too." I glance at his message and can't help myself. I laugh with the incredulity of all this. I laugh again. *A date.* A stinking date. I don't have dates. I have late-night sessions with *Super Mario Odyssey* and *Fortnite*. I have crying fests with my girlfriends over strawberry frosting–stuffed cupcakes. I share a king-size bed with a Lab-hound-husky.

Correction: that's what I *had* over the last year.

A year ago, I'd have retreated. Hell, three months ago I'd have said, *Sorry, I have a date with wine and chocolate buttercream delight.* Even a few weeks ago, I'd have had my guard so far up, I'd have tossed this invitation.

Today?

Today I am *over my ex.*

I fold it in quarters, tuck it into my purse pocket, and meet his gaze.

But just to be sure, I add, "You're serious?"

He laughs but then assumes a very serious voice. "I never joke about being out of practice on dates."

I don't know how dating works these days, but I've never hesitated to learn new things. "Sure, then. What's good for you?"

We agree on a time and a place—Shakespeare Garden, later this week. He waves goodbye and heads into his restaurant.

Once he's gone, I burst into peals of laughter. "I have a date."

And I didn't even have to brave the online dating jungle.

I get in the car, and read the note one more time when an idea strikes me.

Grabbing my phone, I turn on the camera, and record an impromptu video. I do believe I'm ready to date again.

3

CHRIS

Meetings with the boss man are never my favorite way to spend a morning.

But it is Monday, so I suppose it's fitting that I find myself in Bruce's office for our weekly check-in.

He downs a thirsty gulp of coffee then thumps the mug onto his desk, the brown liquid threatening to slosh over. "You sure you don't want some?"

"Nah, I'm doing a cleanse."

He sneers. "A cleanse? You're doing a cleanse? What the hell are you cleansing? You're already at zero body fat."

I laugh, shaking my head. I love to wind him up by pretending I'm 100 percent drinking the California Kool-Aid. To the born-and-bred New Yorker, there's no greater offense than eating chia seeds and downing carrot smoothies for breakfast. "Well, maybe if it's using organic, locally-grown, and hand-picked beans, I can have a cup."

He scoffs. "It's coffee. You drink it. It's good."

I study the mug skeptically. "I dunno. Was it grown within a fifty-mile farm-to-coffee-shop radius?"

"Even better. There's a five-foot radius, since I got it in the breakroom. Are you in or out?"

"Bruce, man, I'm messing with you. When do I ever turn down coffee?"

He shakes a finger at me. "You love to get inside my head." He spins around in his chair, stalks off, and returns shortly with a steaming cup. "Drink it all. It's good for you, no matter who picked or harvested it."

"I will." I take a sip, and it's fantastic.

"All right, enough small talk." Bruce clears his throat and stabs his finger on a stack of papers—the ratings reports from my show on geek culture that streams on WebFlix. Bruce is the new head of programming at the online giant. "This is good, Chris. Better than good. It's almost great."

"Almost?" I arch a brow.

He stares sharply at me. "Great is the gold standard. We're almost there. You're making huge strides after that little bit of turbulence last year."

I privately shudder, grateful that shaky time is behind us, which is precisely where I want to keep it. "Definitely. The rhythm just *feels* better, and I'm glad the ratings are reflecting that."

He raises the papers to his face and smacks a kiss on them. "I love good ratings. Love them like I love a good steak dinner. Like I love a coconut cream pie. Like I love a night out with the little lady."

"All the good things in life. Dessert, romance, and red meat."

He winks. "You know it. And I'm telling you, there's gold in this show. And I know how to mine it."

"With pans?"

He scoffs. "Please. More like with content."

"Oh. *That*," I deadpan. "How are we going to mine for it?"

"Don't you want to know what the gold is?"

"Sure. I love precious metals."

His gray eyes sparkle. He wiggles his eyebrows. He smacks his lips. He is getting ready to make a big pronouncement. "Women. What do you think you could do to attract more women?"

I really love precious metals.

I lean back in the sweet leather chair in his office and flash him a grin, unable to resist the opening. "I could take off my shirt on-air."

He mimes drumming a rimshot, *bada bing*. "You couldn't resist, could ya?"

I shrug happily. "You give me low-hanging fruit, I'm going to pluck it."

"Yeah, well, you can pluck this, kid. You might be Mr. Handsome now, with California surfer charm and a twelve-pack, but it won't last forever."

I glance down at my stomach, hidden beneath my T-shirt. I pull at the fabric. "Are you sure? I made a deal with the devil for these abs."

He shoots me a withering look.

"I don't have a twelve-pack anyway." Softly, I add, "Six is more than enough."

He waves a hand from behind his big oak desk. "Looks fade. Abs fade. You know what remains?"

"Brains?"

He leans forward, narrowing his bushy brows. "Humor, kid. Humor." Bruce calls everyone under fifty *kid*. I don't try to stop him. There's no point. "All right, enough funny business." He rubs his palms together. "Women are the future of streaming. They binge, they game, and they jazz up their phones. All the things you cover in your show. Women are everything. That's what I learned at my last job, and now I'm here to dispense my wisdom to you."

My geek culture show is one of the most watched already on WebFlix, which means it's holy-hell popular.

But the audience is still comprised mostly of dudes.

Bruce points at me. "And I want to make your show soar to the moon." He dives into a rendition of the Chairman of the Board crooning "Fly Me to the Moon," and he's not half bad.

"Bruce, you holding out on me? I need to take you to karaoke night."

He scoffs. "Nah, I have a job. If I start singing, I'd never get a moment's rest from all the groupies. I only have time for making your show the best it can be. That's what I did with Finley Barker, and we're going to take you to Emmy Town too."

I highly doubt my *here's how to beat the game* and *tips for making the most of your laptop* show is going anywhere near a swanky awards ceremony, but it's nice that he thinks that.

I scrub a hand across my chin. "You want me to do more coverage for the games that skew female? Women do have a ton of spending power. They buy all the tech you just rattled off. So the more our female demos grow, the more we can open up ad opportunities here too."

"Ah, it's like you're talking my language. That's music to my ears. So, how are we going to get there on air? Covering mobile games that women play is good. It's a damn fine idea. But what else have you got in that thinking cap of yours?"

"We could dive into workout apps. Those skew toward women but won't turn off our core viewership, like if we started reviewing period apps."

He cringes. "They have period apps?"

A laugh bursts from me. "Dude. Do you know nothing about young women? One of my good friends has a thirteen-year-old, and she tracks every day of the month with an app."

Bruce holds up his hands in surrender and closes his eyes, shuddering. "All I can say is thank the Lord my girls are all grown up and have given me grandkids." He waves a hand, shooing this all away. "Period apps, no. Workout apps, yes. What else have you got?"

"I could look for another gaming expert or tech guru to do some coverage too?"

He nods several times. "That's an option, but . . ."

"But what?"

He holds his hands out wide, like he's drawing a marquee. "I want something out of the box."

Bruce is sharp. The man knows what he's talking

about. When he came to work at WebFlix, I knew my show was in the best possible hands. He's proven that over decades with his ideas, his focus, and his relentless drive.

If out-of-the-box is Bruce's goal, that's what I'll need to find.

4

MCKENNA

I scurry back to my place in Cow Hollow. Last year, as soon as I could, I'd gotten the hell out of the tiny apartment in the Mission that I shared with Todd. One week after he eloped with Amber, the girl child, I'd packed up the whole place with help from my sister, Julia, and my good friend Erin.

I found a new home fairly quickly, thanks to the growth of *The Fashion Hound*. The site curates and sells trendy discount designer clothes and hosts a blog with tips on how to put outfits together. Fashion is my jam, and so is talking.

I do regular video clips that focus on what to wear for different occasions: starting at a new job, a night out with the girls, meeting your man's parents, and—a particularly popular topic—what to wear when you see your Tinder hookup for the first time.

I've been building my business for several years, and an investor plunked in some extra cash last year, earmarked to grow the customer base, especially fashion hounds of the male persuasion. Not only am I a fashion hound, but I'm a working dog, always looking for ways to expand and reach new audiences, and I have a to-do list a mile long that needs to be tackled today.

But first . . . the dog needs a walk.

"So I met a guy this morning," I tell Ms. Pac-Man as we stroll along a quiet block. "I know what you're thinking. Does he carry biscuits in his pocket?"

Ms. Pac-Man wags her tail, eager for an answer, or maybe just a biscuit.

"I wish I knew. I don't know anything about him, but it'll be interesting to see how it goes."

Her tongue lolls out as she trots along.

"Oh, don't worry. I don't want anything serious. When you come out of hibernation, you just want to stretch your legs. You know how it goes."

As we turn the corner, a throng of joggers whips by, so I rein in the chatterbox in me. Yes, I talk to my dog, but it's not as if the world needs to be privy to our conversations. Some things are just between a woman and her best friend.

When we finish the walk and return to the house, I send a group text to the brain trust—my sister and my besties: Julia, Hayden, and Erin—letting them know that tomorrow's scheduled *Game of Thrones* viewing includes a special request from the hostess.

And I add one more text.

Be prepared, as well, for a special screening.

* * *

With my regular appendage on my shoulder—a bag with a laptop and hard drive—I pop over to my friend Hayden's house on Monday evening. She lives next door, which means we share a wall, an entryway, and a front stoop. Her husband, Greg, is out of town, and she's holed up in her home office finishing a legal brief that's due for a client tomorrow, so I help her daughter, Lena, get ready for bed.

I adore Lena for many reasons, including the fact that she loves clothes and fashion and is pretty much the best shopping partner ever. Sometimes, when Hayden and Greg need a break, I happily take Lena out for a girl's afternoon, and we try on everything on Union Street. And I mean everything. The girl has power-shopping genes twined deep in her DNA, and I love that kind of relentlessness when it comes to clothing racks.

Lena waits for me at the end of the hall, pointing excitedly into her room. Her wavy brown hair is unkempt as usual, in desperate need of a brushing. But at twelve years old, she's already learning some of the secret tricks of women. She has pushed it back with a red headband that has big white polka dots on it.

"By the way, I totally approve of the look, but your mom said we have to get you to bed. The girls are coming over soon."

"Look, look, look." She grabs my hand, pulls me into her room, and shows me her find. Their Siamese cat, Chaucer, who's part cat, part Satan, is curled around a teddy bear. "He's cuddled up with my old stuffy. Isn't he the cutest?" Lena hops onto the bed, tucks her feet gracefully under her legs, and pets the demon. She leans her face in to him, rubbing her cheek gently against his downy fur. He snuggles against her, clearly plotting misdeeds. "My mom says he's a trouble-maker, but I don't believe her. He's so sweet to me."

I clear my throat. "Yes, that's exactly what she calls him."

Her mom actually calls the cat Captain Asshole, but that's not for me to repeat. Chaucer is a master of knocking stuff off of other stuff—dressers, tables, shelves. Once, he whacked a vase off the cupboard above the stove, shattering it into a thousand shards. Hayden was real happy about that.

Lena pats her bed. "Can you show me your old videos here?"

I flip open the laptop and trawl through the archives of *The Fashion Hound* on the hard drive, accom-modating her stroll-through-memory-lane request. "Here you go."

We watch several videos as Lena grabs potential outfit combos from her closet, displaying the tween-centric looks for my thumbs-up or -down.

When she finds a yellow shirt with a unicorn leaping over a pot of gold, I jump up from the bed. "I want to be twelve, so I can wear this," I say, grabbing the shirt and pressing my cheek near it. The style doesn't suit me anymore, but it would have fit with tween-me's quirky, sassy, cute look.

Lena giggles. "You can borrow it anytime."

"I wish I could wear this when I meet with

investors. But I'll probably have to wear pants and a starched shirt."

She pretends to barf.

"Exactly."

Crash.

A sharp smacking sound rends the air. I swivel around. My eyes bulge as I stare at the carnage.

Chaucer licks a paw fastidiously as my hard drive lies broken on the floor, the case cracked open.

"Bad boy!" Lena shakes her finger at the cat, scolding him.

He doesn't give a shit. He simply moves on to the other paw.

Hayden rushes in from her office and surveys the damage. "I'm so sorry, McKenna."

I wave it off, because cats can be dicks, and I should have known better, given this dick's track record. "I never should have left it on the bed. What can I say? I was distracted by a unicorn shirt. And hey, this gives me an excuse to visit Gadgets, Gizmos, and Geeks. They can fix it."

She grabs my arm, pleading with big brown eyes. "I promise if you ever need a patent attorney for anything, I'll handle it for free."

"Well, duh. Who else would I go to when I finally invent a website that works without me needing to do a single thing to run it?" I add with a wink then pick up the laptop and the damaged drive.

She laughs and tells Lena it's time for bed, since the other women are on their way over.

I dart back to my place, drop off the laptop on my desk, and return to Hayden's.

After Lena conks out, my sister, Julia, and our good friend Erin arrive. I'll save my news till the end of the show. The four of us pile onto Hayden's couch and catch up on the latest in the saga of dragons and character deaths that leave you reeling.

"Whoa! I didn't see that one coming," I say when a beloved character meets his messy end.

"I did." Erin enthusiastically brandishes the notepad with her predictions. In her triumph, her big red plastic hoop earrings swing wildly around her small, pert face and suit her sandy-brown spiky pixie do.

"Damn." I grab my wine, and Hayden and Julia do the same, all of us imbibing as the drinking game requires.

When the show is over, I tell them it's special bonus-viewing time.

I'm absolutely giddy about my red-hot idea. Nervous too. But definitely excited.

I click on a folder on my phone and show them the short video I recorded yesterday for my blog. I haven't posted it yet because I want to know what they think of it first.

"Hey there, all you fashion hounds and fashionistas. I have a very special edition today. It's a little more personal than usual, but it's chock-full of the best clothing tips." On-screen me pauses dramatically then declares, "It's the best outfit for when you're finally ready to date again after a prolonged time-out."

Julia leaps from the couch, her red curtain of hair flying behind her. She crushes me in a hug while the video plays, detailing my attire when I met the restaurateur. "That's what I wore when I was asked out . . ." I gasp dramatically, leaning into the camera to whisper, "in real life."

Julia lets go and mouths, *No kidding?*

Girl scout's honor, I mouth back.

The video finishes, and I'm engulfed in a group hug. No one has wanted this more than my best friends.

When we manage to separate, we return to the cushy couch where they pepper me with questions.

"When did this happen?" Hayden asks.

"How did you decide you were ready?" Erin tosses out.

I give a quick overview of running into Todd and Amber. They cringe and offer sneers for him and leg pats for me, but I assure them it didn't hurt. "It reminded me that I'm over him. That I'm ready for the next phase."

"And you met someone right away?" Erin asks.

"Yeah, who is this guy who asked you out? The one you mentioned on your vid?" Julia inquires.

"Are you on the apps?" Hayden asks, reaching for her wine with her long arm. Well, both arms are long. She might be part-giraffe. Her limbs are endless.

"Aha," I answer. "That's my grand plan, and I think it's innovative."

"To go on the apps?" Erin asks, deadpan. "Everyone's on the apps, hon. That's how I met Pete." Pete's her live-in boyfriend. "Hate to break it to you, but everyone meets on the apps these days."

I heave a dramatic sigh. "I know. And since it's been, oh, six long years since I dated, I'm a little app-averse." Todd and I met when I graduated from college; we were together for five years. And back in college? No one needed apps. College was one gigantic hookup fest.

Ah, those were the good old days.

"Basically, I haven't dated. *Ever*," I say in a confessional tone.

Erin gives me the side-eye. "Really?"

"I had a couple hookups in college and then a boyfriend my junior year. So that would make high school the last time I actually went on a regular date." I let out a long stream of air. "Damn, that was a long time ago. I've more or less missed the online-dating phenomenon."

"So what's your plan?" Julia asks. "Are you going to do Plenty of Fish or Bumble or Tinder or something else?"

I wiggle my eyebrows, bubbling with enthusiasm. "I'm going to get back in the saddle IRL."

Erin tilts her head, like she didn't understand. "IRL?"

"Yes. In real life."

She rolls her eyes. "I know what the acronym means. But why on earth would you do that? We have better options these days."

"Sweetie, I know you met Pete online. But he's the exception."

Hayden clears her throat. "I met Greg while shopping for a watch for my father. He was shopping for the same watch for himself."

Erin shoots her a *you've got to be kidding me* look. "You met Greg sixteen years ago."

Hayden's jaw drops. "Don't be an ageist just because I'm nearly ten years older than you ladies."

Julia pats Hayden's knee. "Forgive her. She knows not what she does. Plus, we love your wisdom when you share it, and your young-at-heartness too."

"Thanks. I'll be right back. Just need to get my dentures." Hayden rises as if to go.

Erin tugs her back down. "I love you. Just saying, though, you and Greg met before apps were trendy."

"Guys," I cut in. "I don't want to get on the apps. I know there are plenty of successful matches, but I've heard horror stories too. Every woman I talk to has an online dating tale that will scar you. Kara from Redwood Ventures, my lead investor, told me about a guy who tried to talk her into a threesome on the first date. A makeup blogger I know went out with a guy she met online, and in the first hour, he tried to recruit her for his pyramid scheme."

Julia jumps in. "I've heard of that. It's actually becoming a common way for the MLM-ers to bring new recruits in. I hear all those stories, too, at my bar."

I nod. "My point exactly. Besides, I'm more of an old-school gal. I like my old-time music, and I like the idea of meeting someone in real life. Seeing if there's chemistry. So here's my plan—I thought I'd do a little video series. My videos always do best on Insta and online when I make them personal. And I try to be open on those social channels. So why not pair my fashion expertise with dating? It'll keep me motivated to put myself out there."

"Since you're married to work," Erin puts in.

"Work has been faithful to me," I add.

"It's understandable that you'd want to connect your dating quest with business if you can. You're an online influencer. Your Instagram fashion vids get crazy views," Julia points out. "So, you're going to do a what-to-wear-on-dates kind of thing?"

"Well, presuming I find anyone to date. But that's where you all come in." I gesture to the three of them. "I want you to set me up with any single guys you know."

And that's when my friends lose their ever-loving minds. We're talking cheers, hoots, hollers, and squeals that threaten to wake up Lena.

Turns out, there is little a pack of happily paired-off women love more than setting up the single friend.

Erin claps. "Yay! I have been counting the days on my calendar until you were finally ready to start dating again. And maybe to bang again."

"I'll toast to a good banging," Hayden adds.

Julia pipes up. "Call me crazy, but I'm going to toast to you falling in love."

A part of me wants to raise a glass right along with her. To say wistfully, *Wouldn't that be something?* Because, really, that would have been everything I wanted once upon a time. I was born a romantic, and bred a romantic.

But I'm not one anymore.

No thanks.

No can do.

Getting left at the altar has a way of torching all your fairy-tale dreams.

I threw them in a bonfire last year, watched them burn to the ground and the ashes blow away in the wind.

I might have moved on. I might have held my head high. But I am *not* interested in love. No falling, no swooning. Not in any way, shape, or form. Been there, done that, and if I hadn't returned them, I'd have the KitchenAid mixers to prove it.

I am, however, quite interested in having some clever conversations, a few interesting dates, and a good time. I don't even mean in bed. I'm not looking to get laid. I just want to have fun.

"Love isn't in the cards. All I want is to spend some time testing the waters, seeing what's out there, instead of seeing the sad end of my WebFlix queue," I say.

Julia sighs. "It is sad when you get to the end of a binge and WebFlix doesn't even know what to serve you next."

"It's the saddest."

Erin leans in conspiratorially. "I already have someone in mind. One of my massage clients at my spa. He works in advertising, and he's a cyclist. He's on the Lemonhead team or something. He comes in once a week. He has a perfect body. Not an ounce of fat on him."

"I can scope out any of the non-alcoholic hotties at my bar," Julia offers, and I nod my approval, since bartenders meet lots of men. "There are some guys who work at a tech firm nearby who come in for Thursday darts. One of them is quite funny. His name is Nathaniel, so I'll work on him."

"I'll keep my eyes peeled for any attorneys," Hayden offers.

Then, a voice pipes in, small but strong, from the other side of the kitchen. "What about the FedEx guy at your office?"

Hayden whips her head around. "Lena! What are you doing up?"

Lena smiles innocently. "Well, you always say he is cute..."

Hayden scuttles her back to bed, this time shutting the door all the way, and returns to the table.

"So tell us about the FedEx guy," Erin says with a sly grin.

"All the ladies think he's a catch. He has blond hair, brown eyes, and these crazy toned arms," Hayden says, her eyes going a little dreamy.

Reality smacks me with a big old bag of worry-filled bricks. "Wait. Am I even a catch?" I point at myself, and a new dose of fear shimmies down my spine. "What if no one wants to date me? Oh God, I'm an idiot. I'm about to put myself back on the market, and I might get zero takers."

Hayden squeezes my knee. "Enough with that nonsense. Have you looked at yourself in the mirror lately? You're a babe, McKenna. You're tall and thin, and you have great skin."

Erin flicks my hair. "And you have this lush

chestnut hair—which is even hotter than your blonde hair—and crazy, wild bluish-hazel eyes."

Reflexively, I raise a hand, fingering a lock of my hair. I'm a natural blonde, but a month ago, I went darker, eager for a change. Maybe that was the start of my emergence from hibernation. A brand-new color, one that I never thought I could rock.

"The hair change is bold, and you pulled it off," Hayden adds then adopts an over-the-top jealous voice. "And now you're one of those blue-eyed brunettes, which makes you even more rare."

"Oh please," I say, but inside I'm loving the compliments. Correction: I'm loving the *love* from my inner circle.

A hand curls on my shoulder.

"You are McKenna Bell." It's Julia. She's one year younger than I am, and has always been my biggest champion. "You are going to do this. Watch out, men of San Francisco—we have a hot, big-hearted, funny-as-fuck, smart-as-a-whip, and completely awesome woman on the market."

Later that night, I post the video on the *Fashion Hound* Instagram account.

When I wake up, it's gone viral.

Color me surprised.

5

MCKENNA

The closed sign saddens me. I sigh heavily, shoulders slumping, when I reach Gadgets, Gizmos, and Geeks the next day a few minutes before five. I was really hoping to get this hard drive fixed, and the store is supposed to be open till six.

"Crud muffins," I mutter, resigning myself to return tomorrow.

I decide to console myself with some shopping, starting with the electronics store next door, to find a new video game perhaps.

I push open the doors and head to the shelves, taking my time perusing various offerings like *Yooka-Laylee*, which is next to *Super Mario Odyssey*.

I pick up *Yooka-Laylee*, considering it.

"Have you played the newest *Super Mario Odyssey*?"

Before I can even turn around to see where the voice comes from, I laugh.

"Have I played the newest *Super Mario Odyssey*?" I repeat. "Am I breathing? Am I a sentient human being?

I played it, collected a hundred twenty-four moons, *and* saved Princess Peach from Bowser many times over, thank you very much."

I turn to my questioner and Holy Mary Mother of Hotness.

I drop the *Yooka-Laylee* box, and my jaw may fall to the floor too. I contemplate reaching down to pick it up, but that'd make it completely obvious I was checking him out. Perhaps I'll stick to only partly obvious.

My questioner is tall, trim, with wavy light-brown hair and these crazy green eyes that remind me of how Hawaii feels. Well-worn blue jeans hug his legs, and a casual gray Nor Cal T-shirt has the good fortune to cuddle his stomach and chest. The shirt shows off the right amount of tanned, toned arms.

Have I stepped into an alternate universe where hot men grow on streets and in stores, perhaps rappelling down from the planet of Incomparable Babes?

He hands me the box I dropped. "Here you go," he says, and I wish his fingers had just brushed mine. I'd take the barest trace of accidental contact from this specimen.

"Thanks."

He smiles back immediately and then makes a little bow. "Saving Princess Peach many times. Wow."

"What about you? Have you mastered it?"

He waves a hand in the air.

"Oh, c'mon," I persist. "I told you."

"Does anyone really master *Super Mario Odyssey*?"

"That's a rhetorical question."

"But a good one, right?"

"Are you hiding a *Super Mario Odyssey* secret?"

He inches closer, scans the store, and whispers, "Beat the jump rope challenge."

My eyes go wide. "Get out of here."

He just shrugs casually.

I shake my head. "No, that's not how it works," I say playfully, enjoying the exchange with the perfectly handsome stranger behind the warm green eyes, and figuring it'll help me on my dating quest. Talking to a hottie has to be a positive. "You can't just drop a little nugget like that and not give me the goods. Tell me how you did it. Because I can barely get five jumps in."

I listen intently as Hot Guy begins detailing his tactics, talking with his hands, moving his body back and forth, up and down a bit to simulate the way Mario has to keep up with an unpredictable rope. This guy has the kind of arms that women driving cars slow down for, the kind of physique that turns a gal into a gawker. The way his T-shirt falls just so tells me all I need to know about the abs that lie flat beneath.

I remind myself to pay attention, because it's rude to simply stare at his washboard belly instead of his face, especially when his face is so very lovely too. I'm an equal-opportunity gawker. I nod as he shares his gaming secrets, and hope I'm not visibly salivating.

I'm not a gamer geek, but I adored retro games growing up, since my parents used to take Julia and me bowling on Saturdays, and the Silverspinner Lanes boasted all the original arcade games like *Q*bert*, *Frogger*, and, of course, both *Pac-Man*s.

Last year, I took to the console after Todd left.

Games passed the time, but they also distracted me. I got lost in their worlds and was able to escape from mine.

"What other games do you like?" Hot Guy asks, and something about the question startles me. Maybe because it's so normal, and he seems legitimately curious. Then there's the simple fact that we're having a conversation in the middle of an electronics store.

"Scrabble, Trivial Pursuit, Monopoly," I say with a completely straight face.

He picks up the cue easily, raising an eyebrow as he asks, "Clue?"

"Of course. And it was always Professor Plum in the library with the candlestick."

"Interesting. Because Miss Scarlet was pretty wicked with that rope in the ballroom, if memory serves. What about Chutes and Ladders?"

"Let's not forget Candy Land either."

"What was your favorite candy destination in that game?"

"The vintage game, right? Not that new King Candy imitator?"

"As if I'd even be talking about that game," he says playfully.

I'm about to answer when he puts his hands together as if he's praying and says in a whisper, "Please say Ice Cream Floats. Please say Ice Cream Floats."

I laugh with the kind of mirth I haven't felt in a while, the kind that radiates through my whole body and turns into a huge grin. "Of course. I wanted to live in Ice Cream Floats."

"I was all set to build a chocolate and licorice home in Ice Cream Floats. And this reminds me that I need to stock up on the classic games too. But I don't think they sell them here."

"I came here because Gadgets, Gizmos, and Geeks is closed, and that's the only place nearby that actually fixes hard drives." I put on my best sad face. "I was the victim of a cat hard-drive attack."

He pretends to be taken aback. "I've heard of those. How awful."

"It was terrible. Fur, claws, and metal everywhere."

"My condolences. Hopefully you at least caught it on camera so you can post it on YouTube?"

I snap my fingers, aw-shucks-style. "If only."

"Next time."

"Or perhaps next time I will do a better job making sure the hard drive is out of his reach."

He shrugs confidently, quirks up his lips. "Can I see it?"

"Um, sure." Does he have a thing for broken hard drives? I reach into my bag where I have the drive and show him the silver device with the cracked end.

He surveys the damage. "I can fix it."

I give him a quizzical look. "Seriously? You can fix a hard drive? Do you moonlight as a computer-repair guy?"

"Not exactly. I can fix pretty much anything."

"That's impressive."

"Want me to try?"

I study his face, trying to figure him out. "You really want to?"

"I do. Yeah," he says, as if he's digging the prospect of repairing the damaged device. "I really enjoy that kind of challenge. It's kind of like a game to me."

But I don't want to hand over a hard drive to a total stranger. "Actually . . ."

He smiles, raises a finger. "And I bet you probably don't want to give your hard drive to a total stranger."

I shrug, a little embarrassed. "Sorry. But you can't be too careful."

"I hear you completely. But this is simple. And . . ." He inches closer, reaches into the pocket of his jeans, and dangles his keys. Is he going to take me for a ride? "I have the tools right here."

I blink, surprised. "What?"

He waggles the keys, and I spy a tiny little tube that looks like it holds screwdrivers.

"You carry computer-repair tools with you?"

He smiles casually. "You never know when you might need them. I also carry a Swiss Army knife. I read *101 Things a Navy SEAL Knows*." He glances out the window of the store at Chestnut Street, teeming with pedestrians. "And I also know the café next door makes a killer espresso. I'll fix it while we get a cup of joe."

Cup of joe! That's almost like a date!

I mean, it's not a date.

Obviously.

But it's training-wheels time. Talking to this guy as he fixes my hard drive might help me prep for when I go out with Steven from Madcap, the Lemonhead Guy, Nathaniel from Julia's bar, and the other men I hope will come knocking on my door—not literally—once my dating prowess improves.

"Sure," I say, with probably way more enthusiasm than the prospect of a repair job and coffee deserves.

There's a big bonus to this cuppa. I'll get to look at his handsome face while he fixes it. I mean, I'll look at his hands, because the sight of a man using a tool is super hot.

"By the way, I'm Chris McCormick."

"McKenna Bell."

He extends a hand.

We make contact, and there's something about the feel of his strong hand in mine that kind of turns me on. Maybe it's the firm grip, or the way his eyes light up as he smiles. I want to tug him closer and plant a hot, wet kiss on his lips.

Nothing will happen though. He didn't ask me on a date, and I didn't ask him either.

But it can't hurt that I'm thinking slightly naughty thoughts. It's evidence I'm getting my groove back.

Hello, groove. Nice to see you. I've missed you bunches.

6

CHRIS

I'm not checking out her body.

I'm not staring at her face. I'm focused on the task at hand. Thank God I have one, because otherwise, I'd be staring at those eyes. They're blue with gold flecks, making them look almost hazel at times. She has all sorts of colors working in her irises, and the net effect is totally captivating.

So is her lush mouth.

She's running it while I carefully screw the case back together. It's painstaking work since it's tiny and the screwdrivers are the size of nails.

"I tried to fix my shower once," McKenna says, wrapping her slender hands around a cup of coffee. Yes, even her hands are hot. Lord help me.

"Yeah?" I glance at her hands then back at the hard drive. "How'd it go?"

"Well, if you consider scars a good thing, it went well."

I look up. "Scars can be cool. I trust it went exceedingly well?"

She lifts her chin and shows me a thin white scar on the right side of her jaw. "Then I did a fabulous job 'fixing' the shower." She sketches air quotes.

"Looks like it to me. But how exactly did the shower hit you in the face?"

"When the door fell." She says it so matter-of-factly.

I blink, trying to process the enormity of everything that could have gone wrong. "I don't know if I should be impressed you tried to fix a shower door without any fix-it skills, or impressed with your good luck in surviving the incident. Because those things are heavy."

"Hey! How do you know I don't have any fix-it skills?"

I grin. "Lucky guess?"

"Fine. You're right. But what else was I to do?" She shrugs, her tone light and breezy. "It wouldn't close all the way. And that was getting me down because I like to take really hot showers. We're talking sauna temperature. You know the type? Imagine you walk into the bathroom, and steam is everywhere, and you can barely even see the other person in the shower. Just a silhouette. Can you picture that?"

Can I picture it? Hell, I can *feel* that. In my pants. "Yep," I answer, and it comes out a little dry, a little gravelly. Because painting crazy-hot images is playing below the belt, and I bet she doesn't even realize it. Hot women shouldn't use the word "shower" in casual conversation. It's wholly unnecessary, along with "yoga pants" and "strawberries."

"So you tried to fix it?" I ask, forcing myself to focus on the project in front of me, rather than on images of steam rising, which lead to other things rising.

"Yup. And then that shower door showed me who was boss." She holds up her forearm vertically then lets it fall as she makes a *kaboom* sound.

I can't help but laugh. "And whacked you on its way down?"

"Completely whacked. It's kind of a miracle I'm alive, come to think of it."

"I'm glad you survived the shower whacking. What happened with the door though?"

"I called my friend Andy. He fixed it for me. It works like a steamy, dreamy charm now." She takes a sip of her coffee, smiling happily.

I stop and take a drink of espresso.

"Andy? So he's Handy Andy?" I kind of hate him already. Wait. That's dumb. I don't feel a thing for Handy Andy who was in McKenna's shower, that lucky bastard.

"That's a good one. Can you rhyme my name?"

"Henna McKenna?" I toss out.

"And you'll be Chris who brings me bliss by fixing the hard drive," she says, and I just smile at her.

"You're a bundle of energy," I say as I return to my project, moving to the right side of the case.

"And you're a bundle of skills. What do you do when you're not rescuing hard drives from evil cats?"

"Admittedly, that does occupy a large portion of my day. But in the few hours I can eke out, I host a show."

"Like radio show or a podcast?"

I twist the screwdriver a notch. "It's a TV show. On WebFlix. It's called *Geeking Out*."

She narrows her eyes and points at me, circling her finger. "You're a geek?"

"You say that like it doesn't compute, and yet here I am, fixing your tech in a coffee shop. I'd say that makes me a geek."

"You definitely don't look like a geek."

I meet her eyes. They're sparking with a glint of playfulness. "And what does a geek look like?"

"Not like a surfer. You look like you're going to go hang ten."

"I do that too. For fun."

She pumps a fist. "Nailed it. You totally have that vibe about you. Not that I'm pigeonholing you based on your looks. But with the Nor Cal T-shirt, it wasn't the hardest round of *Jeopardy!* to play." She imitates Alex Trebek. "What is the most likely profession of a guy with floppy hair, a not-from-a-salon tan, and casual charm?"

I quirk up the corner of my lips. "You think I'm charming?"

She blushes, but it disappears quickly. "You charmed my hard drive out of my hands."

I screw the final piece of the case back together, set down the tiny tool, drag a hand through my hair, and gesture to the repaired device. "Good as new."

"Wow," she says appreciatively, picking up the drive and gazing at it in admiration. "Thank you so much. You are Mr. Fix It."

I puff out my chest playfully. "Why, thank you very

much. I'm having T-shirts made with that saying. Want one?"

"I do. I want one to sleep in at night."

And there she goes again.

I'd love to linger in this zone, but I'm not getting the vibe that she wants to hang there with me. She's just friendly, and there's nothing wrong with that. I focus on the practical. "It should work perfectly. If it doesn't, call me."

We exchange numbers, and when she puts her phone down, she strokes the hard drive lovingly. "Now I can access my archives when I need to. You're my hero."

She leans forward in her chair and wraps her arms around me, and *whoa*.

Her hair curtains my cheek. Holy hell. She smells delicious, like strawberry shampoo, and it makes me want to nibble on her neck. Kiss her throat. Lick my way up to her ear. Strawberries are my weakness, and so are friendly, outgoing women who are prettier than they realize. That's the kind of woman she is. I bet she has no idea of the effect of her looks. She doesn't play into them one bit.

"I was happy to help," I say, drawing one more clandestine inhale before we separate. Yup, just a hit, and damn, it goes to my head.

I could get high on her.

But I force myself to focus on what she just said. "Archives for what?"

She waves a hand like it's no big deal. "I run a fashion site, and I blog about fashion too. What to wear, what not to wear, that sort of thing."

"Can I see it?"

She shoots me a curious look. "You want to see a fashion video?"

I want to see her video. I want to keep talking to her. I want another excuse to sniff her hair. I guess that makes me a hair pervert. I'll get that on a T-shirt next.

"Yeah, I do. Show me." I egg her on. "C'mon. Show the geek what to wear."

She laughs. "You already dress well. You have mastered the casual California look."

I nudge her with my elbow. "Show me."

She seems to fight off a grin. "If you insist." Grabbing her phone, she clicks over to Instagram, where I catch a glimpse of her follower count. It's half a mil. "You're popular," I say.

"I just like to have fun and post pics. Somewhere along the way, people started following me."

She hits play, and within seconds I can tell she has charisma.

She's funny. She's self-deprecating. She's accessible.

She's exactly who she is—adorable and relatable, and so damn easy on the eyes.

There are no two ways about it. McKenna Bell loves the camera, and the camera loves her. Too bad she's talking about fashion. Otherwise, she'd be perfect on my show. It's also too bad she's talking about other guys in her video and a date some dude asked her on.

All things considered, I'd rather this other dude not date her. Which makes me a selfish prick. But there it is.

"You're a natural," I say, shaking my head in appreciation. And because I *need* to know her situation, I stir up the hornet's nest, referring to a comment she made in her video. "You haven't dated in a decade? How does that happen? You're fun and bright, and despite your predilection for being whacked by shower doors, you're kind of awesome."

"Why, thank you." She takes a drink of her coffee, sets it down, and sighs. But it's not an unhappy sigh. She manages a small smile. "I'm sure you've heard the story before. Girl is left at the altar, licks her wounds for a year, and decides to try dating again, so naturally makes it an online quest, and includes fashion tips too."

Instantly, I hate the guy. I bristle. "Your ex-fiancé is a complete asshole for a million reasons, but most of all because he'd have to be crazy to leave you."

Her eyes are soft. A sheen of wetness flickers over them. She swallows, answering quietly, "Thank you. Thank you for saying that."

"It's his loss, McKenna," I say in a fierce tone. I barely know this woman, but what kind of jackass leaves a woman the day of her wedding?

She clears the emotion from her throat. "It's all for the best. I'm better off without him."

"But he should have figured that out a week or a month before."

"True." She raises her mug and offers it in a toast. "But I'll drink to learning it before I said 'I do.' Besides, one of the biggest red flags was there from the get-go. He liked to steal the first sip of Diet Coke every time I opened a new can. And hello! That's kind of a passion of mine."

I smile at her ability to make light of a difficult situation, lifting my mug and clinking back. "To never stealing first sips." I take a drink of my espresso then ask a question. "And now you're out there and dating again?" The words taste like sawdust.

Or maybe that's jealousy. Which makes zero sense, since I barely know her. Must be a standard territorial guy thing I'm feeling. Yeah, that has to be it.

"I'm kicking it old-school." She slashes her hand through the air, like she's making a *no* sign. "No apps, no online matching, no swipe this or that. I'm going to try my luck the old-fashioned way. I was asked out the other day on the street by a guy who owns a restaurant. Lucky me."

The smile she gives makes it clear she's 100 percent excited for this date, and then some.

"Lucky guy," I say, and I mean it 100 percent.

Her eyes lock on mine for a second, the flecks in them sparkling. "What about you? You must be inundated with date requests all the time."

I scoff. "I'm not on the apps."

"Of course," she says quickly, as if she's correcting herself. "You don't need to be. You probably get asked out when you walk into coffee shops."

She's not wrong, but that's not why I'm not on the apps.

I heave a sigh, and serve up the truth. "I'm honestly not focused on that right now. I have what's known as *trust issues*," I say, trying to make light of it.

"Ooh. Sounds fascinating." She leans closer, her

tone like those used in a 1940s detective flick. "I have those too. Tell me, Chris. What are your trust issues?"

I picture Carly, the producer I dated at work last year. She was fun, ambitious, and fiery. Trouble was, she was also a bit vengeful. "I dated a woman I worked with for about six months. She wanted more, and I didn't. No particular reason, but I just didn't feel the same level of spark. It didn't work out."

"Spark is critical. Or so I hear."

"Spark is essential. I ended things before Carly tried to take it to the next level. She didn't take it well."

McKenna winces. "What did she do?"

My gut churns as I recall the turbulence. "Subtle things. In meetings she'd shoot down all my ideas. On the set, she'd say I was doing everything wrong. She'd claim I missed her emails about how we were doing this or that segment. She'd change up the questions from viewers without telling me. Her mission was to make life as unpleasant as possible, and it worked. I was miserable while she was working on my show, and I don't think I did my best work then, truth be told."

"Was there anything you could do about it?"

I shake my head. "Maybe, but I didn't, which wasn't the best idea in retrospect. There are a lot of people working on the show—writers, other producers, stagehands— who depend on it. But I was so hamstrung and unsure of what to do. I didn't want to rock the boat and cause more problems. I didn't want to misstep and hurt her career."

"Seems like she was trying to hurt yours," she says softly.

I nod, sighing, since that's precisely what nearly happened. "One time we were taking live questions from viewers, and her job was to screen them. She let a guy on who asked, 'Can you give me your best tip for scoring with a girl at work?'"

McKenna's expression goes ashen. "Oh no, she didn't."

"She did, and I was so taken aback by it, I kind of bungled it. I asked her why she let that guy on, thinking maybe the viewer changed up the question. But she said she thought it was a *timely* topic, given all the various dating and girl questions that viewers send in."

"Do you answer them?"

I shrug. "Every so often. Bruce—the head of programming—thinks they're a hoot, so he's been angling for me to do more. But I'm not interested in any of the *best tip for scoring with a girl at work* variety."

"Gee, I can't imagine why you'd dislike that one."

Already I'm digging her sense of humor. "Anyway, the whole experience was an eye-opener. I decided that it's best not to get involved with someone you work with. I've worked too hard to risk it, and there are too many other people who rely on the show. I need to bring my best for every single episode, and if getting involved with someone I work with *might* cause trouble, it's best not to go there."

She nods several times. "Definitely. I do a lot of my work solo, but I have contractors for tons of stuff. Never get involved with someone you rely on to run the ship."

I hold up my mug, and we clink again in solidarity.

She takes a drink then asks, "Where is she now?"

I set down my mug and raise my arms towards the sky. "Hallelujah. She got another job."

"The universe was looking out for you."

"Maybe it was."

"And what about the questions from viewers? Do they still send in the stuff about dates and women?"

"They do. It's weird, since the show has nothing to do with that. But a ton of my viewers keep writing in, asking me for dating advice."

She quirks up her lips. "It's because you're personable and smart and good-looking. They want you to share all that wisdom so they can follow in your footsteps."

I arch a brow, latching on to one awesome adjective. "You think I'm good-looking?"

She laughs and scans the coffee shop, affecting a female newscaster voice. "Bob, did you know ten out of ten patrons at the SassyAss coffee shop think Chris McCormick is good-looking?" She drops down to a male voice. "Well, Susan, I'm not surprised. All the ladies have been checking him out."

A smile sneaks across my face. "Thank you. You're quite entertaining."

"Tell me stuff." She leans in eagerly. "What do they ask you?"

"How do I ask out this woman or that woman? What do I say in this situation? What would I do if this or that happened? How do I know if this girl really likes me?"

She's Susan again. "As I always say, Bob, you can tell if a girl likes you if she invites you home. If she touches your arm. If she laughs extra hard at your jokes, especially if you're not funny at all. But if she does none of that, don't assume she isn't into you. Try, I don't know, being direct and asking her. Women like that, and there's no reason for you to have to wonder."

She says it like she's delivering advice to a guy.

On TV.

On my show.

And that's when it hits me.

I've found my gold, and I wasn't even panning for it. All I have to do is convince Bruce.

7

MCKENNA

He takes off, and I stay behind at the shop to answer work emails on my phone. When I finally pack up, I spot one of the tiny screwdrivers on the floor.

Like when a lady leaves a glove.

Don't be silly.

A screwdriver is just a screwdriver.

I pick it up, tuck it safely in my purse, and smile like a fool because I have a reason to text him.

McKenna: Missing a screwdriver? I'll hold it hostage for you. For a king's ransom, this tiny tool can be all yours again.

He replies as I'm walking home.

Chris: You drive a hard bargain. But I'll liquidate all my assets to get it back. I always want to be prepared to repair hard drives.

As I fashion a comeback, he sends a second note.

Chris: I'm at the studio. I'll text you later, and we'll devise a drop-off plan. Some dark, undisclosed location. I assume you want a leather bag full of unmarked bills.

McKenna: It's like you know me so well already.

* * *

I'm in bed, reading an article on business-growth strategies when Hayden texts me.

Hayden: I'd knock on the wall, but figured this could work.

McKenna: Indeed it does. What's up?

Hayden: I have your next date for you, thanks to my daughter.

McKenna: Are you kidding me?

Hayden: Dead serious. When the FedEx guy dropped off some documents at the office earlier, I arranged a date for you, per Lena's advice. Is that cool?

McKenna: Sure! I suppose I was expecting an attorney, but a delivery guy will work.

Hayden: You don't care that he doesn't have a swank job?

McKenna: Please! This is me! I'm not interested in men for their money. I want a guy who's nice and fun, and who respects women.

Hayden: Excellent. I'll firm up the deets.

I say good night to her and return to my article. A little later, Chris texts. Seeing his name on my phone lights me up in all those groovy parts.

Chris: Just making sure the deal is still on. I have your ransom ready. I just need to know one thing . . . is the screwdriver unharmed?

Smiling, I hop out of bed, scurry to my living room, and take the tool from my purse. I grab a box of ribbons from a cabinet, tie a tiny sliver of one around the tool, shoot a photo, and send it to him.

McKenna: Unharmed, but still bound.

Chris: Please don't hurt it.

McKenna: You know what to do. I'll contact you tomorrow with a location.

Chris: Until then, don't get whacked by any shower doors.

8

MCKENNA

I model a cute Gucci knockoff top for the camera.

"And this is the official what-to-wear-on-your-first-date-in-a-decade look. How did I decide, you may ask? Well, naturally, it only took ten thousand wardrobe changes, but that's totally normal. Just kidding. I don't want you to suffer through all that indecision, and that's why I recommend the simplicity of this top. It's comfortable, simple, and shows off the teeniest bit of skin."

I lean into the camera, showing the slope of my shoulder. "Ooh la la. Let's see if it works. Wish me luck. Don't forget to leave all your what-to-wear questions below, and I will answer them, my fellow fashion hounds. There is never ever a need for a thousand wardrobe changes when you have a fashion hound to help you."

I hit end to turn off the video then raise my face and catch Andy's attention. "What do you think?"

He's parked on my couch, working out of my home

with me today. He gives me a thumbs-up, his standard web-dude response.

"That's why I like working with you. For the wordless thumbs-up," I tease as my blonde half-horse-half-dog trundles on over and parks herself at my feet with a heavy sigh. She's probably counting down the hours until it's time for a walk, her internal doggy clock calibrated to the rhythms of our day. I scratch her ears then pet her head. "Did you like it, girl?"

I do the dog's squeaky voice. "*I loved it. You were so awesome. What should I wear when I run into Roscoe down the street?*"

My jaw drops, and I admonish her. "You naughty girl. You do not have a crush on that beagle. You're bigger than he is."

Andy laughs. "She's a domme, I take it?"

"Evidently. Who knew?" I ask in a hushed whisper.

He clucks his tongue a few times but says nothing. Uh-oh. That's what he does when something's bugging him.

"What is it? What's bothering you?"

"I dunno," he says with a shrug, his curly hair flopping into his eyes as he taps away. "I guess I just don't think this is such a good idea."

"The Gucci knockoff? It's perf. I even modeled it on FaceTime last night for the girls. Erin said it's hot, Julia said it's rocking, and Hayden said she'd do me if she were still experimenting, like back in college. So there. It's a winner."

"Yeah, the shirt's a winner." He tilts his head to the

side and meets my gaze. "I'm not talking about the shirt."

"Then what?"

He heaves a sigh. "I worry about you meeting guys IRL. What if they're stalkers, serial killers, or sadists?"

"Um, the same could be said of guys online."

"Yeah, but that's how everyone does it these days."

"But it's just as likely you could find a creep online," I point out. "Don't you meet creeps online?"

"Grindr is a whole different kettle of fish."

"I thought you were done with that. I thought you were looking for"—I clasp my heart and flutter my lids —"love and a tight bod."

He smirks. "I still want both. But sometimes, I settle for a tight bod."

I grab a pillow from the other end of the couch and toss it at him. He catches it and puts it behind his head. "Look, it's different on Grindr. It's different with guys. We know the score. I worry about you."

"Trust me, I know the score. The score is fun and only fun. This girl doesn't want anything serious."

"But please promise me you're vetting these guys. If you don't, I will."

I grab my laptop from the coffee table, click open my email, and show him the background check I ran on Steven Crane. "See? I'm no dummy. Everything will be fine."

He breathes an audible sigh of relief. "Good. And call me if anything feels off for any reason."

"I promise, Daddy."

He wiggles an eyebrow. "That's what I like the young ones to call me too."

"You're so gross," I say, smiling.

"Fine, they call me Big Daddy."

"Stop, stop!" I shout as I head into the kitchen to grab an apple. My cries are echoed by the phone. It's ringing from the table. "I bet it's that supplier I've been waiting to hear from."

Andy's nearest to my mobile so he grabs it then grins as if he's caught me red-handed. The phone trills again. "Who's Chris? And does this hottie bat for my team?"

A sparkler ignites in me. I spin around and dive for it, hurtling over the back of the couch, landing on the cushions, and wrestling it from Andy.

"Hey there." I try to sound cool, casual, as if I haven't just jostled for the phone.

Chris sighs heavily, his tone dark and brooding. "Hey. I have everything ready. Just let me know when you can do the handoff."

I make my voice gravelly, like I'm a movie thug. "Everything? Don't you be trying to cheat me out of my money."

"Look, lady. All I want is my screwdriver unharmed. No nicks, no dings, and no more choking. I have the dough. That's what we discussed."

"Maybe I'm changing the terms," I say, going full mafia heavy now as Andy regards me like I've changed personalities in front of him.

"Fine. Just tell me what I need to do."

I laugh then drop the ruse. "So, I'm heading to

Shakespeare Garden later. Are you anywhere near there?"

"I started the day at seven so I'm taking off around four to surf, but I can meet up with you before or after. Shakespeare Garden is near the beach."

"Well, I have a date. But why don't I meet you after?"

He's quiet at first. "Sure. That works. When will you be done?" His tone shifts, sounding stiff.

I give him a time, and we pick a place on the beach then say goodbye.

"Eager much?" Andy arches a brow.

"Oh please. He's just a . . ." What is Chris? A guy I met in the electronics shop? The wizard who fixed my hard drive?

"Just a . . . ?" Andy prompts. "Just the guy you were waiting to hear from?"

Yes, that'll do.

9

CHRIS

Shortly after I send the video to Bruce, I have an answer.

Bruce: The answer is yes. And now. And get her.

Chris: That was easy.

Bruce: Some things in life are.

Chris: Okay, so you like her shtick?

Bruce: Like it? I love it. Is that not clear? Do I need to use a megaphone? Stage a parade? Play a trumpet?

Chris: Do you play trumpet?

Bruce: Every man needs a talent. One of mine is that I play trumpet. What's yours?

Chris: Make you money hand over fist with a top-rated show? That's the correct answer, right?

Bruce: Years of training are finally paying off. You got it, kid. Also, when you make me money hand over fist, you make it for yourself too.

Chris: It's a wonderful symbiotic relationship. Like anemone and clownfish.

Bruce: Yeah, sure, whatever you say. Now, go. Or I'll do it myself.

Chris: I can handle it.

Bruce: Then handle it as excellently as I would.

Chris: I'll handle it like I'm playing a trumpet.

Bruce: I'm going to come to the studio and wring your neck. You can't play trumpet for bupkes.

Chris: Oops. Wrong analogy. Like I'm riding a killer wave. Gotta go. Camera is on, and I'm recording a segment.

Bruce: You love to wind me up.

Chris: Only because you are so easy to wind.

10
———

MCKENNA

I'm camped out on a bench in front of Shakespeare Garden, surrounded by the ponds and hills and bike paths of Golden Gate Park. Though Shakespeare Garden has a big name, it's a little spot, maybe the size of a large backyard or a private courtyard. Twin columns frame wrought-iron double gates, a brick walkway cuts across the garden, and a sundial stands in the middle.

I like this spot for many reasons, but especially because Todd and I never went to Shakespeare Garden in all our time together. It's untouched by the enemy.

Steven walks toward me. He is as ridiculously hand-some as he was the other day. He's wearing jeans and a Henley, and I must tell him he dressed well.

His body isn't the only thing chiseled. As he nears me, I admire his well-designed face again, with carved cheekbones, deep blue eyes, and a subtle wave in his brown hair. I take out my earbuds and gently lay my phone on the bench. I smile, a little nervously, and stand. I am not sure what the proper protocol is. I wrack my brain, trying to remember how a first date usually starts, since it's been eons. Entire evolutionary stages, it seems. I could say the wrong thing, do the wrong thing, mess up the secret handshake that experienced daters know.

I err on the side of friendliness, reaching out for a quick, short hug.

"Hey there," Steven says.

"Hi. Good to see you again."

I sit on the bench. He follows suit. I reach for my phone, tucking it safely away in my favorite light-blue Kate Spade. It matches my Gucci-esque shirt and has a playful air. Perfect first-date accessory.

"What were you listening to? Wait. Don't tell." He pretends to be a swami, reading the cards. "An audiobook. I bet you like Kristin Hannah."

"Everyone likes Kristen Hannah," I say with a smile.

"A podcast, then? Something political?"

I cringe.

"Completely agree on that. How about one of those cold-case podcasts? I love those."

I shake my head. "Just music."

He moves next to me. "There's no such thing as *just* music. Music is everything. My ex and I used to love going to concerts."

Hold on.

Did he just mention his ex? In the first minute of a date? I might be rusty, but I feel like that's not how dating works.

"Is that so?"

He nods, a sad smile crossing his face. "Panic! at the Disco. Ed Sheeran. KT Tunstall. You name it."

"How about Adele?" I toss out, a little sarcastically.

He shakes his head, forlorn. "I tried to get her tickets for her birthday. Sold out."

"Wow. She must have been bummed." This is *so* not how dating works. I am so turned off. I don't think I've ever been less turned on in my life.

"Jenny loved Adele." He shakes his head, seeming to snap out of it. "Crap. Sorry. My shrink says I need to stop focusing on my ex. I have to move forward."

Great, I'm his therapy homework. *Go find a nice girl, ask her out, and take her on a date. Prove to yourself that you're starting to get over Jenny.*

He gestures to my phone. "Let me try again. What were you listening to?"

I vow to try again too, to wipe the slate clean. "Billie Holiday. I love her. 'A Sailboat in the Moonlight' is my jam."

"Yes! She's great. 'You Go To My Head,' 'Embraceable You,' 'These Foolish Things' . . ."

Holy smokes. He knows Billie Holiday. I'm so glad I gave him another shot. "Those are my favorites, especially 'These Foolish Things.' That's the best."

He sings a line from the bluesy number, and I croon the next one, and soon we're doing a duet.

This is fun. This is what I missed. This is dating.

When the song is over, I smile. "Look at us. We can totally form a duo."

He smiles, but his lips quiver. His eyes are wet, and

he drops his head in his hands. "Jenny loved Billie Holiday so much."

I sigh, pat his back, and tell him it's all going to be okay and that someday he'll stop missing her so much.

Date number one is officially a bust.

11

MCKENNA

My timing is impeccable.

I do not want to miss a chance to see Chris walk across the sand, so there's no reason for me to be on time when I can be early.

Besides, considering how the therapy session—I mean, date—went, I see nothing wrong with enjoying a little eye candy. After all, I couldn't enjoy the eye candy of Steven. He was unappetizingly soggy with tears.

I park along Ocean Beach, get out of my car, and wait. I try my best to look busy, fiddling with my phone and checking compartments in my purse, but when Chris appears on the horizon, surfboard in hand, wet suit tucked under his arm, I freeze.

I should pretend I'm not watching him. But it's impossible not to. I didn't look away during that scene in *Casino Royale* either, when Daniel Craig emerged from the water. Chris wears board shorts, low on his hips. I watch as he walks through the sand, closer, closer, and there, now I can say without a shadow of a doubt I would like to lick all those water droplets off his chest and his abs and then run a hand down his body to sear into my memory the feel of that firm kind of outline.

He's lickable. He's kissable. He's chat-up-able.

He catches my gaze, and I should be embarrassed. I should act as if I'm not staring, but there's this fluttery feeling inside me, and I want to hold on to it, especially because he's looking at me and not letting go either. Those green eyes of his are the definition of dreamy.

Soon, he's mere feet from me, in all his glistening, ocean-soaked glory, a scratched-up surfboard by his side. Neither one of us says anything for a few seconds, and it's the kind of silence that's filled with unsaid things.

Like, *Can I touch your chest?*

And, yeah, that's probably not cool.

"Hey."

"Hi."

"Thanks for meeting me here," he says, as a wet shock of hair falls across his forehead. He pushes it back.

"Thanks for being a surfer," I say, then I want to kick myself for coming across so googly-eyed.

"No problem." He flashes me a grin and walks to his car. He stows the wet suit in the trunk then slides the board into the rack on the roof, stretching his arms to lock it in place. My God, this is better than Tumblr. This is almost like the best parts of Tumblr weren't shut down.

"I have the bills. You sure you want to do this in plain sight?"

I return to our routine and do my best to stop perving on the man who's already said he has trust issues and isn't dating. "No, man. I'm gonna take you down a dark alley. Now, c'mon."

He laughs, and I reach into my purse and hand him the screwdriver. He clutches it to his chest. "I missed you, little buddy."

"Okay, that's it. Forget the whole surfer mystique. You're one hundred percent geek."

He winks. "Told you so." He smiles then runs a hand through his wet hair. There's something so effortless about the way he moves, so natural. I don't think he's even aware of the effect he has on women. Of the effect he has on me.

I put on my best cheery face so it's not totally obvious I was checking out every single line, divot, dip, and hard-AF muscle in his body. "How were the waves?"

"Great. I surfed, and my buddy Cooper went for a run."

"So you sort of worked out together, and sort of not."

He taps his nose. "Bingo." He clears his throat. "How was your date?" His voice is stiff again, as if the words taste like vinegar. His reaction makes me a little bit happy. Fine, a lot happy. But I'm not ready to let on yet, so I stay in the friend zone.

"Let's just say I had to go home and wash the salty tears out of my shirt before they stained."

He cocks his head to the side. "How so?"

"He spent most of the time crying over his ex-wife."

Chris cringes. "Ouch, that's brutal."

"Indeed. I hope to track down his therapist and demand half of her last session fee."

"Want me to tell her what you did to my screwdriver? That might intimidate her."

"That'd be grand. I'd appreciate that so much."

"I guess this means he won't be getting a second date."

I shake my head. "Nope. But Hayden—she's one of my good friends and my next-door neighbor—has a guy for me."

His jaw ticks, and then he smiles. "Awesome. Hey, any chance we could talk later? I have a business thing I wanted to discuss with you. But I should probably wash the sand off first. Dinner? It's on me."

I'm thrown.

A little flummoxed.

I can't imagine what he wants from me, but I definitely want dinner with him.

So I say yes.

12

CHRIS

"Stare much?"

As McKenna peels off, I turn around to see my buddy Cooper jogging toward me on the sand. He probably ran eight miles, like he usually does.

"Not at your skinny ass."

He scoffs and flexes an insanely buff arm. "Please. There is nothing skinny about me."

He's right. The dude is the starting quarterback for the San Francisco Renegades, and he's fit as a fiddle. As he should be.

He tips his chin in McKenna's direction. "Did she turn you down?"

I play dumb. "What are you talking about?"

"The woman you were gawking at. Hello?" He waves in the direction of her car. "I saw you as I was jogging back. You were ogling her like you wanted to bang her."

"Classy."

"Just like you, man," he says, clapping my shoulder,

his breath coming fast now that he's stopped running. "So what's the deal?"

I shrug, making absolutely nothing of it. "We have a business meeting later. She's a cool gal." Yup, I'm the king of nonchalance delivery.

"Translation: you dig her."

"She was returning my screwdriver."

He laughs, clutching his stomach, doubling over. "That's a good one. That's the best one."

"Whatever." But I'm laughing too. "I fixed her hard drive but forgot a screwdriver."

He holds up one hand, cackling more. "Hold on. I can't handle the sheer level of innuendo in what you just said."

I concede his point. "There is a lot of it in that statement, I'll admit. But why don't you break it down line by line, like I know you want to."

He bites out the words between laughs. "Hard. Drive. I bet you want to—"

"You're such a dick."

He sets his hand on the roof of my car. "Of course I am. And of course you'd say the same thing to me if I claimed I was dropping off a hard drive."

"Speaking of dropping things off, didn't you bring some of your patented chocolate chip cookies to your friend Violet at her hair salon a couple of weeks ago?"

His expression turns stern. "No innuendo about Vi."

I smirk. "Of course. There was nothing more to the baked goods gift. Nothing at all. Nothing whatsoever."

He furrows his brow. "I've known her since I was six.

She's my best friend's sister. And she's awesome. As in, the coolest woman ever."

"Could you make it any more obvious you're into her?"

He stares at me like I've grown antlers. "You're crazy."

I head around to the driver's side and stare at him over the roof of the car. "Like I said, you're into her, and one of these days, it's going to hit you like a ton of bricks. Or like the Dallas D-line sacking you."

He shakes a finger at me as he gets into the passenger seat. "Take that back. Take that blasphemy back."

I hold up my hands in surrender. "Fine. I take it back. You do know I never want to see you sacked."

He exhales. "Nor do I."

Under my breath I mutter, "It hurts my fantasy football rankings. That's why."

He rolls his eyes as I turn on the engine. "And . . . you're a dick," he says, as I pull away from the beach. "What are you meeting with her about? The woman you *supposedly* don't want to nail?"

"I have this idea about having her do a little segment on my show."

"I bet that'll work out real well for you."

"Why won't it?"

"You're into her, man. And you're all about the no-entanglement-at-work rule."

"Then it's a good thing I won't get entangled with her."

That rule exists for a damn good reason, no matter how much I want to nail her. Because there's nothing *supposedly* about that.

13

CHRIS

McKenna shakes her head as she surveys the menu. "I'm in serious trouble with myself."

I lift a brow in question. "Why's that?"

She gestures around us to the hidden paradise of Fritz's Gourmet Fries, tucked away on a side street a few blocks from Fillmore. "How did I not know about this place? I should be shunned. Seriously. Shunned and locked up." She holds out her hands as if I'm going to cuff her wrists. The prospect is downright appealing, and I'm not into that sort of thing. I'm more of a whatever-the-woman-wants-the-woman-should-get guy.

I reroute my thoughts to the topic at hand. "It's pretty bad not to know about this slice of heaven. But then again, I'd like to think I've now introduced you to nirvana."

She slaps the menu on the table with panache. "This is the Garden of Eden. I want it all."

"As I say, you can never go wrong with fries."

"Fries are literally never a mistake."

"Nor are forty-seven varieties of dipping sauces." Fritz's Gourmet Fries is no doubt the best-kept secret. I stumbled across it a few years ago and have been addicted ever since.

McKenna scans the list of sauces I've already memorized—pesto mayo, spicy yogurt peanut, creamy wasabi tapenade, spicy lime, roasted red pepper, and so on.

"They all sound delicious." She sounds as if she's in a trance. Her blue eyes are hazy with fry-sauce lust. "Which is your favorite?"

"If I told you my favorite French fry dip was ketchup, would you think less of me?"

She stares at me as if she's studying my face. "One, I wouldn't believe you."

"Is that so, Doubting Thomas?"

"It's impossible to like ketchup best when you have all these choices, especially when you can have creamy wasabi tapenade. Say you're sorry. Say you're sorry right now for that slight to the world of clever sauces."

Laughing, I lean back in my chair. "Fine. Sorry, sauce," I say, like a kid who's not sorry, but is forced to apologize. "But wait till you try the ketchup."

"It's just ketchup."

I shake my head. "Nope. It's not just ketchup."

"What is it, then? Magical elixir ketchup?"

"Sort of." I lean in closer and drop my voice to a dirty whisper. "It's sinfully good."

She nibbles on the corner of her lips. "Like, orgasmically good?"

Holy hell. She went there, and I like it. The way she

says that word, like it's intriguing and fascinating, is a jolt of lust delivered straight to my groin. Then again, it'd be pretty hard for her to say "orgasmic" and for me not to be aroused, so c'est la vie. "Yes, it's orgasmic ketchup."

She turns, raises a hand as if talking to the imaginary waiter, then adopts a French accent. "Garçon, I'll have a dozen ketchups, s'il vous plaît. With ten to go." She turns back to me, drops the accent, and with a straight face, explains, "One can never have too much orgasmic ketchup."

I stroke my chin. "Hmm. I believe I saw that on a bumper sticker the other day."

"Words to live by." She peruses the menu once more then sets it down and gestures to my shirt. "Now, don't get me wrong—your surfing outfit was great, but I like the casual yet classy look of your attire."

I tug at my polo shirt. It's some shade of green. "Why, thank you. I wasn't entirely sure if polo shirts were still acceptable for a sort-of-kind-of business dinner, so I'm glad to have the fashion hound seal of approval."

She mimes stamping the shirt. "It definitely works. The jersey cotton gives it just the right casual feel, and the celery color is perfect for your eyes."

That was quite a thorough assessment, but then, it shouldn't be a surprise. "I had no idea it was jersey. Or that celery is a color. What color is celery?"

"The color of your shirt, of course. It's a very pretty green."

I slide into a feminine tone. "Oh, thank you so

much, so glad you like my pretty shirt." I return to my regular voice. "And you look great." It comes out a little awkward, like I shouldn't be complimenting her, and maybe I shouldn't be, given my detour into dirty thoughts of removing her shirt a few minutes ago.

The pink button-down looks like it's made of the softest material ever, thin and kind of sexy but also classy. It gives a little hint of skin and makes me want a bigger peek.

She shoots me a smile. "Thank you. It's the ideal outfit for fries, I believe. But then again, everything goes with fries. You could eat them in a boat, you could eat them in a box, you could eat them with a fox—" She covers her face with her hands. "I can't believe what I just said."

Laughing at her unexpected Dr. Seuss segue, I point at her. "You're reciting *Green Eggs and Ham*!"

"I know." She looks up, a little embarrassed. "Well, Chris. The cat's out of the bag. I'm kind of a dork."

"Nah, that's just a good book. But would you eat them in a house? Would you eat them with a mouse?"

"I will eat them in a boat, I will eat them with a goat," she fires back.

I slam a fist on the table. "And I will eat them in the rain. And in the dark. And on a train."

A waiter pops by our table, fresh-faced and sporting a smile that stretches to Timbuktu as he sets water glasses on the table. "And what can I get you fine folks today?"

"We're going to go a little wild and order some French fries," I begin.

"Yeah, go nuts!" the cheery fellow replies. "What kind of sauce would you like with those?"

I meet her gaze. "Tell the man."

With a Cheshire cat smile, McKenna straightens her shoulders, clears her throat, and announces in a prim, proper voice, "I'd like to try the orgasmic ketchup, please."

The guy rolls with it, giving her a thumbs-up. "Right on. That's exactly what it is. Come to think of it, we should rename it Orgasmic Ketchup."

"Come to think of it indeed," I add drily.

He cackles, McKenna laughs, and I take a pretend bow.

"And what other flavors of sauces would you like with your fries?"

I gesture to the lovely brunette across from me. "McKenna, want to go full ladies' choice?"

Her eyes sparkle with delight. "Actually, I love surprises." She turns to the happy dude. "Why don't you surprise us? Just pick your three best, any three."

The waiter's smile spreads, as if he's thrilled to have been entrusted with such an important task. "It will be my pleasure to hand-select the sauces."

In addition to the fries, McKenna orders a Mediter-ranean salad, I opt for a chicken sandwich, and we return to the conversation.

"Are you a closet Dr. Seuss fan?"

"No, I'm loud and proud on that front. But it was at the top of my mind because I read it to my friend Hayden's daughter the other night. She's twelve going on eighteen, so she's totally over it, but she was amused her younger self liked it." She taps her chin. "I believe she considered it an *ironic* reading of the book. And you?"

"It was my little sister, Jill's, favorite book growing up, and I taught her to read way back when, so I have it memorized."

Her smile widens. "What a good older brother. Is she your only sibling?"

"I have an older brother. He works in London. And Jill's the youngest. She's in New York. She landed a part in a new Broadway musical called *Crash the Moon*. It opens soon, and I'm going to see her opening night. I'm really proud of her."

"I've heard about that musical. It sounds amazing. Davis Milo is the director," she says, then hums a show tune that sounds familiar, probably from Jill singing it. "That's from *Anything For You*, another one of his shows. He's a genius."

"Jill says the same thing. She's pretty stoked. What about you? Any siblings?"

"I have one sister. Julia," she says then tells me about the bar her sister owns in the Mission District.

We segue into favorite drinks, then favorite shows, and before too long it occurs to me that I could easily spend the whole time talking with her and never make it to the reason I asked her to dinner. She's so damn easy to have a conversation with.

But I need to focus on business affairs, not dating affairs that aren't real. Once more, I recalibrate. "The reason I asked you here is that I have an idea. It's a little crazy. A little edgy, but it's also one-hundred-percent legit awesome, and I hope you're up for it."

She rubs her palms together. "You want me to hold other tools hostage?"

Yeah, like my dick.

Whoa, where did *that* come from?

Oh yeah. Maybe the filthy thoughts that keep jostling their way to the front of my brain.

"Sure, I have a wrench that's been naughty. Maybe you can put it in its place?" I joke.

"I'm prepared to kidnap it if need be. But, in all seriousness, what do you have in mind?"

I'm flying blind here. I've no idea if she'll be interested in my proposal, but I have a gut feeling she'd be awesome at it. Plus, Bruce went bananas for her videos and insisted I get her, so here I go. "Would you like to do a dating segment on my show?"

She freezes, mid-drink of water.

Her elbow doesn't move. Her lips are parted. She stares at me as if I'm speaking backward, a record played in reverse.

She blinks and sets the glass down. "You want me to do a segment on your show? Me? A fashion gal? On your show on geek culture?"

This may be harder than I thought. But I go for it, making my case. "You're a natural on camera. You're funny and personable and chatty. And I thought it would be great if you came on to tackle some of the dating questions the guys send me. You already answered one at SassyAss, and it was brilliant."

She laughs, a nervous undertone to it. "And because

I nailed one answer at the coffee shop, you want me to answer more on *Geeking Out*?"

"We're trying to reach more women, and even though the questions would be from guys, you have such a natural appeal to both men and women that I think it would help us expand our viewership."

"But I'm not a dating expert," she says, flustered. "I'm sort of the opposite."

I need to make it clear that's what I want. That's her charm. "That's perfect. You don't have years of polished answers that a so-called *relationship* expert could give. You speak from the heart, and you'd be speaking from your experiences out there as you date again. You could talk about what went right and what went wrong on your dates, and answer questions." I push past the gravel in my throat from thinking about her dating. It honestly shouldn't bother me so much. I do my best to wrestle the tic of annoyance far out of sight. "Sort of like reporting from the front lines."

"Dating is definitely the front lines," she says, and it sounds like she's considering my proposal, like I'm getting her close to the yes both Bruce and I want. "But, Chris, you really think I'd be an expert?"

I make an impassioned plea, locking my gaze on hers. "I don't want a shrink or a Dear Abby. I want a real woman who's putting herself out there. Who speaks honestly and openly. I don't want someone giving canned advice my viewers can find in any magazine or *BuzzFeed* piece. I want someone in the same situation my viewers are in. Dating again, figuring it out."

She tucks one strand of hair behind one ear then

another. "And it would be questions and sort of a 'what works' thing? Like what I'm doing now for my site with fashion, but more focused on advice to men?"

"Absolutely," I say with enthusiasm, because I can feel her bending. "And, to be completely frank, you have an audience. I want you and your audience."

"Greedy man," she says as if she's chiding me.

"I'll give you my audience if you give me yours," I say, dangling another carrot.

"Ooh, I love it when you talk business growth." Her eyelashes flutter.

"I can talk business growth all day long."

She lifts a brow. "You surf, you're handy, you're a video-game expert, you're the Pied Piper of geeks, and you like business strategy. You're too . . . fabulous."

I straighten my shoulders, preening. "That's me. Fabulous."

"Seriously. How do you know all this stuff? Business and video games and fixing stuff?"

I tap my chest. "I was a double major. Business and software design."

Her eyes sparkle. "Me too. Business and English."

The waiter appears with our salads, sandwiches, fries, and sauces, asking if we want to know which ones he picked.

She shakes her head. "I'm all in when it comes to the sauce surprise."

"It's like Christmas morning."

The waiter deposits the plates on the table then clasps his hands together, almost like he's praying. "Now, can I get you anything else?"

She shakes her head, and I say no. After the waiter leaves, I point my thumb at him. "Is he the happiest person you have ever met?"

She whispers, "Clearly he's eating all the ketchup."

I waggle a fry in front of her. "C'mon, you know you want it too."

She moves in closer and opens her lips, and damn, she has the sexiest mouth, with pink gloss and lips I want to kiss. But I'll have to settle for feeding her a French fry.

She takes it and does an obscene eye roll that shoots electricity through my blood.

What the hell? I'm turned on by a woman eating a French fry.

Forget trust issues.

I have lust issues.

She moans as she chews, places a hand on her chest, flutters her eyes closed, and finishes the fry in the most sensual way any person in history has ever finished a French fry.

She opens her eyes. "Ohhhhhh."

And I've got a screwdriver right here. With a hard drive. "Good?" It sounds like I'm talking through sandpaper.

"That is indeed orgasmic ketchup. You better have some."

"Bring it." I'm like a moth to a flame. I can't resist flirting with her. I part my lips as she swipes the fry in ketchup and feeds it to me. I don't think I can top her sensual fry-eating finesse, so I simply chew and declare it delicious.

She adopts a skeptical frown. "I don't know. I don't think that fry did it for you, Chris." Somehow she says my name like it has five syllables and is the sexiest name that's ever fallen from her lips.

"Fine, give me another." She dips one more in a wasabi-style sauce and offers it. I lean in closer and groan as I take it. Her eyes widen at the sound I make, at the rumble in my throat.

Holy shit. Am I affecting her? By French-fry-eating? I'll stuff them all in my mouth if that turns her on.

She swallows a little roughly, as if she's catching her breath. Maybe I am getting under her skin.

Which is exactly what I shouldn't try to do. But hell, it's too fun.

I finish chewing. "Pleased now?"

"Seems like you were."

"I was indeed quite pleased."

"I think we just turned this meal into a hands-on session in foreplay with French fries."

"Foreplay is my favorite game."

She laughs, then waves her hand. "Time to behave. And this now concludes today's edition of Chronicles in Stimulating Fry-Eating."

I laugh, take a bite of the chicken sandwich, and return to business. "What do you think? Are you game? I think you'd be awesome at it. And obviously, we'd strike some sort of deal so it's beneficial for you as well."

"Actually . . ." A glint of an idea seems to cross her eyes. "I've been weighing this as we eat."

"Whoa, you're a multitasker."

"Yes, I can think and eat and talk all at once. And I think we can do this as a promotional deal."

She's piqued my curiosity even more. "How so?"

"Why don't we cross-promote? It can be more of a marketing or promo partnership. I'm trying to expand and reach guys. This could be a good chance to reach some male viewers about the fashion looks I'm curating for young men."

I beam, loving the way this is coming together. "That's perfect. We want to reach the young female market. You want to connect with young men. Boom. We both get something out of this. Why don't we do it for a few segments and see how it goes?"

"I'd love to. And maybe you'll find some of my audience likes to play games."

"A lot of young women do. The female gamer is one of the fastest-growing demographics in the whole video-game business, and of course, women are avid consumers of tech in general. And you're clearly into games, since I met you when you were debating which new one to buy."

"I blame *Q*bert*."

"That wily guy is responsible for your love of games?"

"He's completely the culprit. I kicked ass at *Q*bert* when I was a kid. My parents were totally into this retro bowling alley near our house, and it had all the classic arcade games."

I reach for a fry and dip it into a lime-ginger sauce and listen to her talk.

"I used to play for hours, bouncing from square to

square, level to level. The noises, the snakes, the green magic balls . . . I miss *Q*bert*. And I mean the real *Q*bert*, with the diagonal joystick, the pixelated graphics, the funky sounds."

Like I have an ace up my sleeve, I grin at her. "How badly do you miss it?"

"A ton." She tips her chin at me in question. "What's the devilish little smile about?"

I lean back, all casual and cool as I drop news I think she'll love. "I have *Q*bert*."

"For the PlayStation, you mean?"

I shake my head. "I have the real *Q*bert*."

"The arcade one?"

"The real deal. In my living room."

She practically does a jig in her chair. "I'm so jealous right now. I'm having visions of eighth grade, me acing the round, punching my initials in for all the world to see."

I wiggle my eyebrows. "Bet you can't beat my high score."

"Oh, you think you can take me on in *Q*bert*?"

"I do."

"You're on. Someday I will take you down. Wait." She slaps a palm on the table. "That might be a fun thing to do on a date—play video games. I could do a bit on what to wear on a gaming date."

"See? It's already coming together. You have to do that as a video blog for your site—a gaming date. And then when you come on my show, the guys will have tons of questions about gaming dates."

We make plans for her to come to the studio. I hold

out a hand to shake, and from the French-fry-feeding to the orgasm talk to the way I stare at her lips, I wonder what I just got myself into.

I've just signed her on to be a part of my show when I want to get my hands on her.

Except that's a limited assessment of the broad range of McKenna and the way I'm starting to feel for her. There's more to it than wanting to touch her. I want to get to know her better too.

And I'll have to resign myself to that and *only* that— talking. It's smarter that way now that we're working together.

If anything happened, I'd be rolling the dice on damaging what I've built with *Geeking Out*, and I can't chance that.

We spend the rest of the meal discussing business.

After we finish, we walk down Union Street. I glance briefly at her hand, and in a flash of temptation, I want to take it, thread my fingers through hers, and experience that first touch.

I'm tempted to make that small start. A sweet little touch that's innocent but could lead to so much more.

I squeeze my hand into a fist so I can resist reaching for her. "You know something about those fries?"

"What about those fries, Chris?"

"I will eat them in the rain. And in the dark. And on a train. And in a car. And in a tree."

"They are so good, so good, you see."

I should stop flirting with her, but evidently I like to play with fire.

14

MCKENNA

That evening, I close the blinds in my bedroom and slip into bed with my laptop, settling under the covers. It's been a few hours since my dinner with Chris, and I know one thing for certain: I didn't want the evening to end.

Maybe it's because he's easy on the eyes.

But maybe it's because he's so easy to talk to.

I've only seen him three times, but each time we seem to fall into a fast and comfortable rhythm. Like we can talk about anything, and we do.

When I'm with him, innuendo seems to tumble from my lips. Orgasmic ketchup? Where did that come from? And I didn't stop. I kept up the routine. But then, he seemed to run with it. He seemed to like it too when I took the fry from him.

Maybe that's simply because he wants us to work together. Perhaps his flirty charm was because he had a proposition for me.

And it's a downright appealing one.

Focus on work. Work is steady. Work is reliable.

I click open my business plan for the year ahead to center myself. Right there are my top goals: expand the reach, and reach more men. Chris is paving a potential path for me, and it's best if I laser in on that, not on how much I want to trade words and tango with double entendres and get him to make that sexy, carnal groan again when he's eating a French fry.

Oops. I went there.

Must not go there again.

Besides, even if there was a chance of a little something more, how would it fit into the plan we just detailed? It wouldn't. So there's no more need to noodle on it.

Done.

Over.

Finito.

I resolve to focus on the new promotional partnership, and only that. I'll even prove it to myself right now. I grab my phone, open the text thread, and write a message.

McKenna: I'm excited for our partnership! Thinking about it A LOT. I bet some of the women who watch my show might want to try a little *Guitar Hero.*

I hit send, proud of myself. Because that game rocks. Well, it did last time I played it.

I slide out of bed to brush my teeth, trying to remember when I was last slashing notes and pretending to be a guitar god. Once my choppers are scrubbed and buffed and clean as can be, I turn off the light in the bathroom then the bedroom, telling myself not to check my text messages. Instead, I pop over to the dashboard for my site, pleased to see the audience numbers are rising quickly for my dating segments. My first outing might have been a bust, but Kara from Redwood Ventures will enjoy these numbers.

She's not the only one. I happen to be a big fan of audience growth too.

Ms. Pac-Man wanders in, bats her big brown eyes at me, and waits for my permission. "Oh, stop pretending. I know you get on the bed when I'm not here. I've seen your fur all over my comforter."

I pat the bed and she jumps up, flopping down beside me.

Hmm.

When *was* the last time I played *Guitar Hero*? Was it in college? Oh shoot. Did I just commit a massive faux pas?

I grab my phone, stabbing at the message like there's suddenly a recall button on my text app, wishing I could take it back.

Chris: Hate to break it to you, but that game isn't even made anymore. Sorry to be the bearer of bad news.

McKenna: Moment of truth—I actually tried to reach

into the phone and retrieve the message. Just picture me digging my hands into the ether of cellular bandwidth to cover up my dorkitude.

Chris: Hey! It's all good. I didn't expect you to be the keeper of gaming facts. That's my job.

McKenna: And you're excellent at it. Turns out, the last time I played it was in college. But I do recall having a blast then.

Chris: No surprise. That game is insanely fun. The game-maker tried to reboot it a few years ago, but it didn't go over well. Too bad, because it's like one of those classic old-school games. I've been to a few arcades that have it.

McKenna: Whew. Glad I haven't made an absolute fool of myself.

Chris: No way! Actually, now you've got me thinking about *Guitar Hero*. And wanting to play again.

McKenna: And evidently I want to play it too.

Chris: Then we will remedy this. How about a lesson after your first segment?

I furrow my brow as I glance at the snoozing blonde

beast. "He wants to give me a lesson, girl. What do you think?"

She lifts her snout.

"You obviously approve."

Her tail twitches.

"You completely approve, and I need to get on that, stat? Is that what you just said?" I gasp in shock. "Ms. Pac-Man, how dare you?"

Her tail thumps harder.

"I do not want to ride him like a horse," I mutter. "Fine, maybe for a minute. Okay, longer. But this can only be business. He doesn't get involved with people he works with."

I drop a kiss to her snout. "So just do the lesson as friends and business partners, and don't think all those naughty, dirty, wonderfully delicious thoughts? Is that your final advice?"

I do her high-pitched voice in response. "*Yes, sounds brilliant.*"

The dog oracle has spoken. I write back.

McKenna: You teach at the computer store?

Chris: That's why I was there when I met you. Once a month, I teach newbies how to play video games. Like you, evidently. Go ahead and say it. I am a full-fledged internet geek.

McKenna: You are, certifiably. Sounds fun though.

Chris: We'll have a good time, and I promise I won't be too hard on you.

McKenna: It's okay. You can be hard on me.

I force myself to turn off my phone for the night. When I snuggle under the covers and close my eyes, I'm thinking about Chris more than a business partner should.

But you know what?

It feels good to let my mind drift to how hard I want him to be.

So good, in fact, that his message the next morning feels like a flirty, dirty reward.

Chris: If you insist, then, I'll be prepared to be quite hard on you.

15

MCKENNA

Before I leave for my dinner date, Hayden stops by, eyeing my outfit. "You look fabulous. Is this the new Bershka?"

I glance at the red-and-black leopard-print blouse with a tie front. "Yes! Isn't it yummy? It's the most versatile top in the world. In fact, that's what I said in the video I just posted."

"It's gorgeous," Hayden states, touching the soft fabric. "It's the kind of top you can wear to work and then to a date."

"Gah! When you say stuff like that, it makes me feel like you love me," I say playfully.

"Goofball. I do love you, and I know fashion is the way to your heart. Well, fashion and dogs."

"And naturally, Ms. Pac-Man appeared in my Insta video." I bend down to rub her soft head. "You were such a good companion."

She wags her tail, and my phone buzzes with a message that my Lyft driver is here.

"I'm off! And thank you for setting me up with Dan," I say, mentioning the FedEx guy who services her office. "Wish me luck."

She blows me a kiss. "Luck, but you don't need it. Be yourself, and have fun."

I slide into the Lyft, and as the driver takes me to a restaurant in Russian Hill, I answer questions from viewers on Instagram and on my blog. They ask for advice on what to wear, and a few want to know how the dates are going.

Briefly I picture Chris, then I want to slap my mind. I'm not dating Chris. Please. He's off-limits.

I reflect back on teary-eyed Steven, and I devise a diplomatic reply.

The first one was interesting. He was hung up on his ex, but so it goes. I'm undaunted and dipping my toe back in the pool again tonight!

After I answer a few more questions, I arrive at Lemongrass, a hip new place wedged between a coffee shop and another coffee shop, because . . . San Francisco. I thank the driver and push the door to head inside.

A man is there, holding the door open. "Are you McKenna?"

"Yes, that's me," I say, a little flustered because holy cannoli. Dan Duran is handsome. He has blond hair and brown eyes, a combo I love.

"Great to meet you." He extends a hand, and Hayden was right—the man has strong arms. Maybe not quite as toned or muscular as Chris's, but still, they'll do.

Stop. Do not think of Chris on your date.

He guides me to the table and pulls out my chair.

My heart beats a tick faster since he's so darn polite. "Thank you."

He sits across from me. "Glad we could do this."

"Me too. Also, I have to say Dan Duran is a fun name."

He crinkles his nose. "Thanks. It's kind of goofy."

"No, not at all. It's happy and upbeat. It's a great name."

He smiles. "I'm glad you think that. It's alliterative, and kind of rhymes in multiple ways."

"Exactly. That's why it's fun."

Now I'm not thinking of Chris at all, because Dan Duran is a cool guy. We chitchat as we review the menu and discuss what we're going to have. When the waiter comes by, Dan remembers my order and places it for me—mushroom risotto with snow peas.

I want to pump a fist because this date is starting off so much better than the waterworks one.

He gestures to my top. "That's pretty."

"Why, thank you. It just arrived, and I'm already a little bit in love with it." Yes, this date is worlds better. Everything is working.

He squints, studying my appearance quizzically. "But . . ."

I barely have time to brace myself.

His voice is clandestinely sweet as he says, "I wouldn't let you wear that out with friends."

I blink, shaking the water from my ears. Surely they must be clogged. What did he say? "Excuse me?"

There's that deceptively affectionate tone again. "It's lovely for a date with your man, but you can't wear that if you're out with friends or going to work."

I force a laugh because surely he's joking. "You're right. I'll save it for the house." I practically slap my knee so he knows I'm totally in on it too.

He clucks his tongue. "Good. Because it's too appealing. I don't mind that you're wearing it on our first date, because you don't know better."

I slam on the brakes. "I don't know better?"

He smiles, and it's not sweet. Not even saccharine. It's condescending. "That's only because we just met. But now you know how I feel. And I couldn't let you dress that provocatively if we're together. Other men would be drawn to you."

The number of things wrong with what he's saying are nearly too high to count, but I start simple. "First of all, if I'm with someone, I'm not drawn to other men."

Dan shakes his pretty head adamantly. Why, oh why, do the good-looking ones have to be so kooky? From Steven to Dan, the universe is drawing wildly handsome cards for me and then turning them into complete wackadoodles.

"Of course you wouldn't be drawn to other men. But men are animals, and I wouldn't want to put you in that position."

"Gee. Thanks for the chivalry."

He smiles, thrilled I finally understand, simple-minded female that I am. "Exactly. A man's job is to keep a woman safe, to make sure she's treated wonderfully, and to ensure no other man would even attempt to go near her."

"Perhaps a leash could help in that regard?"

He chuckles. "A leash is hardly necessary if you're wearing appropriate clothing. Only I'll know what's underneath. Not the whole town. Have you considered turtlenecks for daily wear?"

I cringe, every fashion-loving bone in my body mortally offended. I am two-hundred-six-bones-worth of pissed at Dan Duran.

But just to be completely, absolutely certain he's not putting me on, I ask, "You're definitely not joking?"

His face is stony. "I'm serious."

I paste on my best smile as I fold my napkin and set it on the table. "Thank you, Dan. I appreciate your candor. And the mushroom risotto sounded delightful. But I'm afraid I have a low-cut top and tight jeans to wear when I saunter around the city tomorrow." I adopt a frown, like I'm abjectly sad at this turn of events. Then I dip my hand into my wallet. I toss two twenties on the table. That'll cover both of us.

"Goodbye, Dan Duran. This girl dresses herself. And sometimes, call me crazy, I pay for dinner too."

I walk out.

* * *

"How can I put this tactfully? He wasn't exactly a raging feminist," I tell my sister as I take another drink of my Purple Snow Globe, a new drink Julia is testing out on me. I'm at her home away from home, Cubic Z in the

SoMa neighborhood, where she tends bar. With raspberry juice, gin, and sugar crystals on the rim, this drink is exuberantly delicious. "And I don't need a feminist per se. But he was more like the anti-feminist."

"He didn't pull out your chair or hold the door?"

I nod savagely. "Jules, he did all that. The problem was he wanted to do that and put me in my place," I say, then explain what went down at dinner.

Julia mimes dropping a ball then kicking it far, far away. "Ouch. No man is winning a Bell woman with that attitude."

I place the martini glass on the counter and look straight at her. "Exactly. And even though I'm not looking for a boyfriend, and I'm definitely not looking to get serious"—I flinch momentarily at the memory of how such a relationship could go belly-up in one fast weekend away in Vegas—"I don't want to date someone who thinks he's better than, oh, say, my *entire gender*."

Grabbing a cloth, she wipes down the bar, nodding in solidarity. "I hear ya, sister. R-E-S-P-E-C-T is where it's at. I see no reason to waste time with any guy who doesn't see eye to eye on such basics." She tosses the towel onto a hook. "But it does raise some interesting questions. Have you thought about what happens when you go on a few dates with someone who does see eye to eye with you?"

I take another swig of the heaven in a glass, savoring the sugary finish. "What do you mean?"

"I know you're into the whole 'let's see how this goes and have fun,' which is awesome, and exactly where you should be at. But what if the next guy tickles your fancy, curls your toes, and stimulates your mind. What then?"

I part my lips to answer, but I don't have a quick retort. I want to have fun, to get back out there, to test the waters. But I haven't considered beyond a date or two, maybe more. My heart won't let me. I still have a cage around that organ, protecting it from pain. It's still bruised and tender to the touch.

That's why I need to keep everything on the surface level. A few dates can't hurt me. If I meet someone I like, I'll simply keep it in check.

A customer at the other end signals he needs a refill, and Julia tells me she'll be right back. I glance briefly at my sister, who is quite simply a heartbreaker. She's sexy and curvy and has that kind of reddish-auburn hair that drives men wild. I bet someday some man is going to walk into this bar and sweep her off her feet.

But me? Being swept away? That's hard to conceive of, especially when I'm zero for two at the dating plate.

Zero for ten in the toe-curling department.

And that's A-OK. I don't need my toes curled and my fancies tickled. All I need is another way to meet interesting men. I glance around the bar, and an idea strikes me. I could take a class. A mixology class. Or a cooking class. Or a cupcake class.

When Julia returns to my corner of the bar, I'm lit up like a bulb. "I should take a class. I can meet potential dates there."

Her lips tip up. "Yes! I heard someone talking about a coffee-tasting class recently. Why don't you try that?"

She gives me the name for one, and I google it and sign up on the spot.

Pleased with my can-do attitude, I set my phone on the bar with a flourish. "Take that, Dan Duran."

Julia holds out a palm to high-five me. "Also, why don't we do a girls' night out? We can go to some hip bars on a Saturday night, and you can meet guys that way."

"Boom!" I thrust both arms in the air. "I love it."

She taps the bar. "And someday you're going to meet someone you have an instant connection with." She snaps her fingers to demonstrate then heads over to a new customer.

I flash back to Chris, to our easy conversation over fries, to the moment at the beach, to the store, to the coffee shop. There was something sort of instant in our connection, wasn't there? We have the kind of quick banter and repartee that makes a girl think of possibilities, of days and nights and music and laughter. It makes a girl think songs were written for her, like "A Sailboat in the Moonlight," my favorite Billie Holiday number.

Every now and then, I wonder what it would be like to find my sailboat in the moonlight. To find it for real.

As I take another swig of Julia's concoction, I let myself linger on my text messages with Chris, scrolling through our last conversation. Our saucy comments and naughty replies.

I stare at the exchange, running my finger across our messages.

Wondering.

Waiting.

Hoping.

But what am I hoping for?

Just as soon as I ask the question, the answer touches down, landing softly but insistently before my eyes.

I see a kiss that starts sweet and soft and slow. Hands cup my face as if he's claiming me, saying *you're mine* with his lips. I imagine a thumb tracing a line along my jaw.

And I see myself melting into a moment that makes my toes curl.

I halt the image train. I can't let the fantasy go any further. After all, I'm seeing him tomorrow for work. I finish my drink and resolve to enjoy this newfound friendship and partnership with him.

That's all there is, and that's what I focus on the rest of the night as I go home, kick off my shoes, and strip out of my clothes.

Except I'm pretty sure it's not in any business handbook to think of your new colleague the whole time you're taking a hot shower.

But I do it anyway.

16

MCKENNA

I choose my outfit carefully, opting for a cap-sleeve mint-green blouse with a sweetheart neckline and capri jeans. I shoot a quick video for my Instagram, detailing why I chose it for my first on-air segment, then posting it with details on where to nab the goodies.

I head to the studio. Chris waits for me in the lobby, looking California cool in jeans and a navy Henley.

"I'm pretty sure those clothes were made for you," I say, after he gives me a quick hug.

"These? Nah, I just grabbed them at Banana Republic, or maybe even Target, I think."

I nudge him. "It was a compliment on how good you look. Not on where you shopped."

"Oh." His cheeks turn a faint shade of red. "Thanks."

"You're blushing!"

"Thanks for pointing that out," he says as we turn down the hall.

"It's kind of cute actually."

"Thanks, that's what I was hoping for. Cute blushing."

"You don't like the sound of *cute blushing*?"

"It's not very manly, now is it?"

"A man doesn't have to be manly every second of the day," I say softly.

He looks over at me as we walk, adopting a too-deep voice. "Yes. Yes, we do."

I roll my eyes. "I like your blushing. It's sweet."

"Great. Now I'm sweet," he says sarcastically.

I shrug happily. "I think it's sweet that you blush at a compliment."

We reach the end of the hall, and he stops abruptly. "You look completely fucking edible."

I blink, and my cheeks flame. "I do?"

"You do," he says with a devilish grin, then he leans closer. "And now you're blushing, and it's insanely cute too."

I smack his arm. "You devil."

He winks, sets a hand on my back, and says, "Let's do a segment, like the couple of cute blushers that we are."

Yup. I can't stop flirting with this man.

And from the looks of it, he can't seem to stop flirting with me either.

That makes me deliciously happy.

17

CHRIS

McKenna is a pro. With the cameras on us, she makes everything seem easy. And honestly, this is her baili-wick and mine too—chatting it up for the lens.

I introduce her and explain what the new segment is all about, then I point to the camera. "And now it's time for *you* to have your say and get all your burning questions answered." I turn to the gorgeous brunette by my side. "Are you ready, McKenna?"

She rubs her hands together. "Bring it on. Hit me."

"No softballs here. We have a question from Jason in Dallas. This is a tough one. When you're on a first date with a woman, what does it mean when she orders lobster?"

She looks at the camera then at me. "That's simple. It means she likes shellfish."

I give her a playful look. "C'mon. That can't be all it means. Isn't lobster like a code for something?"

She pretends to consider the question then answers thoughtfully. "Yes, it's code for the lady likes shellfish."

She turns more serious. "Fine, let's be frank—it's usually the most expensive item on the menu. A lot of times guys think that means it's a guarantee for action. Am I right, Chris?"

I hold up my hands, so I'm not culpable for that kind of one-track-mind thinking. "I'm not saying I think that, but some dudes do."

She pats my shoulder. She's quite touchy, and I like it. I like it a lot. "It's okay," she says. "If you ever take me out, I promise I won't order lobster."

She's perfectly playful, and that's what I want. When I prepped her for the segment, I told her to feel free to ad-lib, to poke fun at me, and to have a good time. That's what she's doing, and it feels natural.

"Fine, so no lobster when I take you out, but let's help Jason. Does it mean anything or nothing?"

"In all seriousness, what it means is something awesome. Are you ready for it?"

I dig in my heels, wiggling my fingers for her to serve it up. "I'm ready. We're ready. Give it to us."

"It means she likes you enough to not be embarrassed eating in front of you. A lobster is a big, messy production. Take it as a good sign that she's into you."

I pump a fist. "Woot woot. She's into you, Jason."

McKenna holds up a finger. "But don't take it as a sign she wants to get busy."

"Fair enough. All right, McKenna. You ready for one more question?"

"As I'll ever be."

"Patrick from Seattle is curious: how do you get

back into dating after a long-term relationship went kaput?"

"Ah, you're speaking my language, Patrick. I hear you. I get you. And there's one thing you need to do."

"Tell us what that is."

She meets my gaze. Her blue-gold eyes are tinged with a hint of sadness, but also a strength that's incredibly alluring. She's had the shit kicked out of her by love, but she's back in the saddle. That's bold, and bold is hot.

"You have to put yourself out there," she says. "And you do that by saying yes to things. Going to a class, or learning a new skill. In my case, I asked my friends to set me up with any single guys they knew."

"Did you have any basic requirements?"

"Just kindness. I think there's a mistaken notion that women want a man with a big wallet or a hot body, and hey, there's nothing wrong with either. But kindness matters more."

So few people say that, and I couldn't agree more. Still, my viewers want me to be entertaining, so I do bicep curls, mouthing *But a hot bod is a nice bonus*, as she continues.

"But I simply said to my friends, 'Set me up.' Here's a hint—women love to set up friends on dates. Patrick, if you work in an office, let the married women know. And trust me, they'll have dates galore for you."

I turn back to the camera. "There you go, Patrick. You heard the woman. Put yourself out there. Boom!"

When the segment ends and the cameras go dark,

Bruce strides in, all dapper in a three-piece suit with gelled-back hair that screams *Mad Men*.

"Hey, Dating Wizard, that was fabulous," he croons to McKenna, dropping a kiss to her cheek.

"I'm so glad you liked it."

"Liked it? I loved it. Loved it like I love the surf-and-turf special at Ruth's Chris Steak House. And now, for some reason, I'm craving lobster. Thanks for that."

I laugh. "You should go indulge, but don't expect anything from the shellfish."

He shakes a finger at me. "I expect nothing, Turkey Legs. That way I'm pleasantly surprised when I get anything."

I jump in, explaining his ways to McKenna. "By the way, a nickname means he likes you."

"Then I'm happy to be known as Pumpkin Pie and to keep working with you, Turkey Legs. Also, nice to meet you, Bruce," McKenna chimes in.

"It's a complete delight to meet you," Bruce says, then turns to me. "By the way, I heard from Zander Kendrick's manager. Says he'd be up for an interview soon. He'll call you to set it up."

I pump a fist, then look at McKenna. "Zander Kendrick is a game designer. I've been trying to get an interview with him for ages."

"That's awesome," she says. "Good for both of you."

Bruce tips his imaginary hat and exits. When he's gone, she says, "I like him. He's old-school and cool."

"You like old-school?"

"I like hot new fashion and old retro tunes and meeting people in person. I'm eclectic."

"Let's go play an old game in person, then," I say, and usher her out of the studio, grateful that my time with her isn't ending.

And hopeful, too, that the time ahead is as good as all the other times with her have been.

18

MCKENNA

In the game room at the store, Chris hands me a black plastic guitar. I strap it over my shoulder, and my neckline slides. Darn it. I fiddle with the hemline, pulling it back into place.

Chris moves in closer, whispering, "Nice try. It's only slightly distracting when you do that."

I hide a wild grin at the compliment, even as hot tingles sweep down my arms. "Far be it from me to distract my tutor."

He shoots me a grin that's equal parts sexy and sweet.

Chris turns on the Xbox and hits the on button on my guitar.

The game whirs on—a dark-pink mountaintop set against a black night sky appears on the gigantic television screen hanging on the wall in front of us. Chris moves closer to me and taps a few buttons on my guitar to click past various screens. His nearness is heady, and he smells like sunshine and ocean breezes.

I bet he tastes like sunshine and his hair feels like a warm breeze.

Since I haven't played in a while, we review the basics, how to play the green, red, and yellow notes on the easy level of the game. How to hit them at just the right time. How to hit the strum bar at the same time too. I butcher my way through "Slow Ride" and "Hit Me with Your Best Shot," getting booed by the virtual audience and tossed offstage. I dig in like a batter at the plate; eyes fixed on the screen; feet planted firmly; index, middle, and ring fingers poised over the keys. Chris walks behind me, adjusts the strap a bit, moving the guitar a little lower. His right hand hovers over mine, flipping my concentration upside down and inside out. I'm not used to this feeling, electricity meets longing, and I don't know what to do with it either. The last time I felt this way was in another lifetime, when Todd and I were planning a wedding and a future together.

For a sliver of a moment, I'm back in time, remembering our relationship. Todd was the same in those last few months as he was when I met him—charming, funny, philosophical. There were no signs, no indication that his eye would wander, that his heart would leap over the fence and run away without even waving goodbye.

The only sign, I suppose, was his Diet Coke trickery. He knew about my first sip fixation, but he would always ruin it for me by opening the can himself and taking a hit with a devilish little smirk.

But if that was it, how can I read anything into anything? Or something into nothing?

That's why I can't trust signs.

Or feelings.

Or flirtations.

It's safer to date for fun.

And this right now? This is fun.

Even though it's not a date, not a date, not a date.

"Okay, you want my top tip?"

At Chris's question, I return to the present. And this is where I want to be. Here, with this wickedly handsome man whose hands are on mine, whose body is behind me, and whose lips are near my ear.

"I do," I say, a little more breathlessly than I expected.

"This may sound cheesy, but the real key is to let go. Let go of the need to check where your hands are or to look constantly at the neck of the guitar. Can you let go?"

I want to let go with you. Give me your top tip for that. Show me how that feels. "I'll try."

"Close your eyes."

"Close my eyes?" My tone is tight, a little nervous.

"Yes, close your eyes. I know it's going to be really hard for you not to be in control for one second, but trust me."

"Oh, ha ha," I tease. But the thing is, I do trust him. That awareness hits me out of the blue, but it's a fully-formed realization. I trust him. "I trust you," I whisper, as I close my eyes.

"Good. That's what I need," he replies, his voice soft

and a little tender. "Try to *feel* where your fingers are. Here's the green note." He places his finger down on top of my index finger, playing the green note.

Sparks zip down my chest.

"Here's the red." He presses his middle finger against mine, playing the red note now, and the pleasure ricochets through my body, on a mad dash to fill me with silver-and-gold sensations, all from his touch.

"And here's the yellow." He keeps his ring finger against mine, playing the yellow note. His scent floods my nostrils. The muscles on his arms bump up against my softer parts. His lips near my neck, so incredibly close, are thrilling.

I feel. Dear God, do I feel.

I feel a zing and a zip and a whole lot of tingles and shivers.

I want to lean into him. I want him to wrap his arms around me and hold me tighter as he teaches me to play. I want contact. I want it so badly, I don't know how I'll ever play a song because I am living and breathing only one thing right now—the wish to be closer to him, my back curved against his front, his arms wrapped tight around me, our bodies entwined. I'm a tuning fork, vibrating hotly from his touch.

"What you want is to *feel* the notes, not look at them."

I played arcade games for fun when I was a kid, and for release when I was left curbside by my ex. But I never imagined video games as foreplay. Here with Chris, every single second feels like a slow burn. Like we're giving in to whatever flirtation we've been having.

Like he's going to turn me around, place his hands on my cheeks, and pull me in for a kiss, the kind that makes the world fall away.

Is that how he'd kiss? Like my sailboat in the moonlight?

He leans in even closer and whispers in my ear, "You can open your eyes now and play."

I inhale deeply and let my eyes float open. I feel wobbly from the way he's touched me, from the way I've let my thoughts spin into a dark and dangerous place of possibility.

I press start on Poison's "Talk Dirty to Me." I hit the green notes, then the red notes, then the yellow ones. Then the next set and the next. I even nail a long note, then another, then a whole sequence of *star-power* notes, and I give in to the game. I channel all my desire into the playing, and I'm jamming here, the pseudo-music taking my mind off the fact that I want Chris to talk dirty to me.

The last note sounds, and the crowd on the screen goes wild. I raise my hands in the air. *Victory.* A thrill rushes through me. "I rock!"

Chris smiles big and wide, the teacher proud of his student. "Fast learner are you," he says in Yoda's voice.

"You're a Star Wars geek too."

"You know it," he says proudly. "You want to play some more?"

I nod vigorously and then spend the next hour knocking out several more songs and even making it through my very first guitar battle, where I own the guitarist from Rage Against the Machine after two tries.

By the time we turn off the game, I'm feeling pretty energized, and I also don't want this time with him to end.

I draw on my newfound mantra: *put yourself out there*.

It's not a *date* I'm about to suggest.

But even so, I go for it with gusto. "Do you want to grab a bite to eat? There's a great taco shop around here. I don't know if the quesadillas are orgasmic, but some might say they're swoon-worthy."

He grins, and it lights up his face. "Let's go get some swoon-worthy quesadillas."

I take him to a hole-in-the-wall taqueria with orange Formica booths and countertops and a menu that's half-English, half-Spanish. We order chicken quesadillas to share, and he asks if I want a Diet Coke.

My eyes widen. "It's like you're speaking my secret language."

He taps his temple. "I listen, woman. I definitely listen."

He turns back to the woman at the counter and orders two sodas.

"I can't let you caffeinate alone," Chris says to me.

"How gallant of you to join me in the caffeination quest."

The woman gives us the cans and glasses, and we carry them to the table.

After we sit, he slides one can toward me. Then the second one. His eyes twinkle with mischief. "Would you like to open both cans?"

I squeal inside with delight. "You, sir, are a gallant

knight indeed." I sigh forlornly. "But I can't. I want you to enjoy the fun too."

He lifts a brow. "Let's do it together."

And like the dorks that we are, we crack open our cans at the same time, chuckling as we take our first sip, then pour them into glasses.

"So, have you always been a knight in shining armor?" I ask, keeping up with our little routine.

"Sir Galahad McCormick—that's what they called me in high school."

"Speaking of, where'd you grow up? You have to be a California native. You've mastered the whole dark-blond-and-beautiful look."

There's that smile again. Magnetic and adorable. "Beautiful?"

"Oh please. I've already complimented you fifty ways to Friday since the day we met. You're hot. There. Full stop."

He tilts his head, staring at me as if he's drinking me in. "You're beautiful. Full stop."

My heart trampolines in my chest, and a smile threatens to take over my whole face. Before I start tap-dancing and singing in the rain, he picks up the thread.

"I'm from Brooklyn, of all places, but I hate the cold, so I got the hell out of town for college."

"Where was that? When you double-majored," I add, so he knows I definitely listen too.

"I went to Stanford."

"Stanford?" My jaw drops. "You went to Stanford?"

He laughs. "What? Just because I'm not wearing a pocket protector or a business suit?"

"I didn't mean it like that. I was just surprised. I guess because you're so laid back. You're the video game guy; you're hip. You don't seem like a Stanford guy. You're more Berkeley."

"Despite them being our rivals, I'll take it as a compliment. But it's all true—I studied software design and business."

"What'd you do after graduation?"

"I landed a job designing video games," he says as the waitress brings us the quesadillas. Chris thanks her, and she leaves. "I did that for a few years and then decided I wanted to do my own thing. I started consulting, doing business strategy and whatnot for companies in the gaming space. I was asked to speak at conferences, then started video blogging, then the video blog turned into a TV show. And here we are now."

I kick my foot back and forth under the table, enjoying his story. "And here we are now indeed."

"And you, McKenna Bell?"

I tell him my story, that I grew up in Sherman Oaks, went to college at UCLA, spent a few years at the fashion brand Sandy Summers, then launched *The Fashion Hound* with Andy's help. "Now I'm here, somehow giving dating advice on your show. Life is weird. And it's all because a cat broke my hard drive."

"I owe that cat a drink," he says then takes a bite of quesadilla.

"I'll let him know you're game for a boys' night out." I take a bite of my own.

He smiles, then his face turns serious. "So, how did

your second date go? Did the dude break down and cry, curl up in a fetal position, or ask you to change his diaper?"

"Eww!" I cringe, shrinking away. "That's horrible."

"If you think that's horrible, consider yourself lucky. I've heard some hair-curling stories from the single mom who lives down the hall from me."

"There was no diaper changing. That's a hard pass," I say, then fill him in on Dan Duran and his notion of a woman's role in the home.

"I suppose it would be a bad idea, then, for me to tell you that if we dated, I'd expect you to cook all the meals and do all the cleaning?"

He's so straight-faced as he says it that I grab my napkin, ball it up, and toss it at him. He catches it easily as I answer him, "And just for that, you're in charge of all chores if we date."

"Fine, I accept. But only if I get to pick the restaurants we go to."

"You're so controlling in our fake-dating world. Where would you take me?"

He stares up at the ceiling as if deep in thought, then his eyes meet mine. "Besides all the finest taquerias and coolest French fry establishments, I'd take you to karaoke and comedy clubs and arcades. But I'd also go shopping with you, if that was what you wanted. And I wouldn't complain or sit on my phone the whole time. I'd dutifully check out every outfit, and I'd enjoy every second of it."

The zip returns, and it's multiplied. It's quadrupled. It's a supersonic burst of delight winging through me.

"This is not fair. You're making it too fun to fake-date you."

"It would be fun," he says, and the air goes quiet and still.

Is he testing the waters? Is he trying to say we should truly put ourselves out there? I don't know that we're going there, but I know I want to dip a toe in.

"It would be fun. It's always been fun with you," I say.

He smiles back at me, his sea-green eyes sparkling, reminding me of a secluded island cove. I don't seem able to break the gaze, nor does he, and now it's more intense, stealing my breath away. He looks at me as if he wants to know me, wants to see inside me.

It's exhilarating, but so damn risky, so I tap the brakes. "The only issue with putting ourselves out there is that we work together."

He nods, a bit solemnly. "It's true. That makes everything risky."

"And then there are those pesky *trust issues*. I know I sound like I'm making light of them, but they're weighty."

He nods. "Yeah, they can be. For both of us, I presume. Do you think you'll always have your concerns?"

I shrug, a little sad. "I hope not. What about you?"

"I probably should let go of them, but I don't have the time to focus on that right now. Work has to come first. Know what I mean?"

"I do."

His hand slinks closer to me. "But if we dated, I'd

try to. If we dated, I'd just want to have fun, since I know that's what you want."

Oh God. What I want now is him. I want him to shove that plate of swoon-worthy quesadillas aside and make *me* swoon, not just with words, but with his hands and tongue.

"That's what I want. Just something light and easy," I whisper.

"I could do light and easy, if we dated," he says, scooting closer, his thigh now touching mine. I die from pleasure, every single molecule in my body turning liquid. I don't want to ride the brakes any longer.

"I could do the same," I say, and I'm aflame, lit bright from longing.

He gazes at me, his voice low and husky. "You know what I'd do next in this scenario?"

"Tell me." I wait on the edge of desire for his answer.

19

CHRIS

I could say I don't know what comes over me. But that'd be a lie. It'd be a weak-ass cop-out too. I do know what comes over me.

Desire. Lust. Want.

Sometimes it's that simple.

We're teasing and toying, playing at the edge of a game. But I'm a gamer, and I know sometimes you have to go for it. You jump off the cliff, you run into gunfire, you rocket-launch into the stars.

You don't know what's on the other side. You don't know if you'll make it to the next level or die a brutal, pixelated death.

You know the risks, and you do it anyway.

I've wanted to touch her since I met her. That's how attraction works. I knew it in seconds that day in the store, and I've wanted her more and more every time we've connected. Every time I see her, talk to her, text her.

I can feel the heat from her body. I can smell that

strawberry shampoo that drives me wild. "I'd run my hands through all this luscious hair," I whisper.

Her breath hitches.

My skin sizzles.

Lust grabs hold of me. I thread my fingers through the silky waterfall of chestnut strands, and she's a cat, arching her back, purring under my touch. *This* woman. My God, I want to be the one to show her what it's like to be wanted.

"Don't stop," she murmurs.

It's a plea, and there's a warm buzzing sensation taking over my body. Wait. It's way more than warm. Make that white-hot. "And if we dated," I say as my fingertips trail down her neck and she trembles against my touch, "our first kiss would surprise both of us."

"Why's that?"

"Because we wouldn't expect it to happen today . . . now," I whisper, and her lips part. Her eyes blaze with a desire that matches my own.

"I definitely didn't think it was going to happen now." She grabs my face in both her hands and yanks me toward her, and I laugh, loving, absolutely loving, how much she wants this.

But I want to kiss *her*, not the other way around.

"Let me kiss you," I say.

She lets go of me, huffs, grumbles, then commands, "Fine, but do it now."

"If you insist," I say, cupping the back of her neck.

"I insist." She shudders, and that's another thing about McKenna I note and file away. I put it in my drawer of Absolutely Awesome Responses to Kissing.

My lips brush hers, tasting her sweetness, and her want too. She tastes like she's vibrating, humming with the need to get closer.

She murmurs as I sweep my lips over hers, and that sound sends a jolt of lust down my spine, making me picture all sorts of permutations of that sound and possible next steps—grabbing her hand, taking her out of here, taking her to my place, having my way with her, making her feel so damn good.

Like she deserves.

Like those idiots she's dated so far could never make her feel.

The thought of other guys even having the chance to kiss her rouses the caveman in me. I ratchet up the kiss, harder, deeper, like I'm telling her with my lips that this could lead to hot, late, dirty nights.

But I know this is only hypothetical, like we're playing a game.

I know in a bone-deep way we aren't going there today.

I know today is for first steps, for testing, trying.

Breaking the kiss, I pull away slowly, taking my time so I can register the look on her face. Her eyes are hooded, hazy; her lips are bee-stung and parted.

She's the image of longing, and I want to take her home.

"So . . ."

"So," she says, her breath uneven.

My lips curve up in a crooked grin. "That's what it would be like if we dated."

"So now we know."

"Now we know," I echo.

I know we can't go there, we got caught up, but I want to know what could happen next, and what the hell this means. Except, I don't think I'm going to get those answers. Sometimes you have to hit pause in the middle of a game instead of playing on.

That's what we do when the waitress shows up a few seconds later, asking if we need anything else. We pause, and I tell the waitress just the check, and McKenna and I instantly return to work chatter, talking about how today went.

It's easier than saying *Wow*, or *Let's do that again*, or *So, should we try this thing?*

I don't say those words, nor does she.

Maybe neither one of us knows what we want to happen next.

Correction: I know what I want. I just don't know if my wishes make any sense.

I ignore them, pasting on my best *let's have fun working together* face. "So, Miss Rock Star with the dating answers, any type of questions in particular you want me to find for you to tackle in the next segment?"

She purses her lips, gazes at the ceiling, then seems to find the answer. "I was thinking I could answer questions about how to meet people in real life these days. I can talk about the girls' night out I have planned for this weekend. We're going to The Tiki Bar on Fillmore. It's such an old-school way to meet someone, but I kind of love it and am curious if it still works. And I have a coffee-making class too. I thought it would be a great way to meet new people. And maybe some new guys. Don't you think it's a good idea?"

It's a horrible idea. I swallow past the stone in my throat. "Yeah. Sounds like a great plan."

"Don't worry." She pats my arm and shoots me a sweet, tempting grin. "If we were dating, I'd cancel it."

I nearly jump on that. My lips and tongue are ready to say *Cancel it now*.

But I remember Carly and all the shit that went wrong when our plane sputtered to the ground.

A voice in my head says, *You have trust issues.*

Another voice says, *Time to get over them, dickhead.*

I'd like to take her out.

I'd love to do this again.

But by the time I'm ready to ask – *What if we just went out on a date?*— McKenna has moved on to other topics, and I don't have the chance to reveal how seriously I want her to cancel her class.

Or maybe it's better I don't take the chance.

Because I'm not so sure if that's what she wants me to do.

20

MCKENNA

I should be upbeat.

This is going better than expected.

What were the chances I'd not only nab a parking spot right outside my coffee-making class, but master the art of making a latte and, on top of that, snag a date?

Slim.

But slim chances paid off, and maybe my dating karma is throwing down the gauntlet to compete with my parking karma. Because the goddesses of dating have delivered J. P., the chatty, goateed, aspiring coffee-maker I was paired up with in the two-hour class. When class ended, he asked me out, and here we are, ordering a drink on a Thursday evening at a bar.

"Let me guess—you're not in the mood for anything coffee-based," he says, a smile crinkling the corners of his lips.

"And you guessed right. How about a martini?"

"Coming right up," he says then orders.

We make small talk, and I learn more about him. He's twenty-five—yay, me, for appealing to a younger man—studied communications in college, and works as an assistant director for a sports marketing firm.

So far, he seems—dare I even think it? —normal.

No rampant sexism. No rivers of tears.

It's my responsibility, then, to make the most of tonight, even though a part of me is elsewhere, and I don't know how to graft it back in.

But I try. I'm a trier. I'm the go-getter, the plucky gal who swings back against heartbreak. I focus on my date, his kind brown eyes, his thoughtful expression. "Tell me more about what you do. Sports marketing sounds fascinating," I say, swinging my foot back and forth like I did with Chris. Maybe that'll make me feel the way I do when I'm around him.

J. P. beams, eager to share his passion, it seems. "I love it. I love every second of it. I love to ski and hike and bike and run, and I love the chance to market races and triathlons . . ."

He continues telling me about his work, and it's interesting.

I swear, it's truly interesting.

And he's completely friendly.

Wonderfully engaging.

I try desperately to focus on every word.

But a big chunk of my brain is back in time, replaying yesterday.

That kiss. That absolutely delicious, decadent, toe-curling, bone-melting, mind-bending kiss.

That was the reason kissing exists—for kisses like

that. A shiver runs through me at the memory that feels less like a memory and more like my body is living it again.

I actually feel that hot rush of golden sensation cascading over my shoulders as I replay the kiss. It's on repeat in my mind. The way his hand curved around my neck, the way he lingered on a strand or two of hair, stroking it, touching it. How his lips devoured mine. Pleasure slams through my body like I've hit the hammer at a carnival.

What the holy hell?

"And that's my goal," J. P. says as our drinks arrive.

Ashamed I've no clue what he said, I do my best cover-up, raising a glass. "Let's toast to meeting and exceeding goals."

Not to remembered lust.

He clinks his glass to mine and asks me about my goals.

I have so many. Normally I get so excited about business and the site and blog, but right now, my number one goal is to figure out what went wrong at the end of the swoon-worthy quesadillas.

Yet I'm pretty sure I know what went wrong.

He didn't tell me to cancel my class today.

And I would have. I would have canceled the class in a heartbeat. I was waiting on the edge of my orange plastic seat in the taqueria for those words to rush past his lips.

Cancel your coffee class. Cancel it and go out with me.

That's what went wrong. I've started to want something I can't have. Because Chris doesn't date women he works with.

Drinks with J. P. lasts another forty-five minutes, and it's fine. Everything about it is fine, except for my stupid mind, stupidly wandering to places where it shouldn't go.

* * *

"Maybe I should call this dating thing off." I flop down on Hayden's couch later that night.

She lifts an eyebrow. "Because of one bad date?"

"Three. Well, tonight's was good. I was bad."

"What happened?" She settles in next to me.

I bury my face in the couch pillow, muttering, "I was a bad date. I was distracted."

"Ah, what distracted you, kitten?"

I grumble and mumble, "I like someone."

She hums. "Didn't see that one coming when he posted a snippet of the segment."

I yank the pillow off my face. "What? You could tell? From a snippet?"

She scoffs, petting my hair. "You're so cute."

I toss the pillow at her. "Stop. Are you serious?"

"Yes," she insists as she crosses one long leg over the other.

"How?"

She cackles. She howls with laughter. "You're hilarious. You have it bad, wanting to know if it's obvious."

"Well? I'm waiting." I twiddle my thumbs.

"You guys have this great chemistry. But more than that, it's sort of a charm, a sweetness. I feel as if I'm watching two people flirt."

I groan. "That's the worst thing you could have said."

"Why?"

"Because it's exactly how I feel with him. All warm and bubbly. Like a delicious soda you crack open. And it's effervescent, and you want to taste it so badly."

"And how does his soda taste?" she asks, in an Elvira-type purr.

"Like the best soda ever. Obviously."

She smiles like she has a secret. "This is good, then."

I shake my head, popping her bubble. My own has already been pricked. "He doesn't get involved with women he works with. He made that clear the first day I met him, before we started working together. It's just a rule of his. Do I know how to pick 'em or what?" I flip over and frown. My sad face sags down to my knees, and I hope I look so pathetic that Hayden will take pity on me and bake me her spectacular butterscotch cookies.

"Well done then, Fashion Hound," she says sarcastically, patting my shoulder as Chaucer saunters by.

I point at the Siamese. "It's all his fault. If he hadn't knocked down my hard drive, I'd never have met Chris, and then I'd never have felt all this *conflict*." I say the last word on an epic moan.

Hayden turns to the cat. "Evidently everything is always your fault."

He meows saucily and turns the corner into the kitchen, leaping onto the counter. A sound like ceramic hitting tile rends the air.

Hayden sighs. "Looks like he attacked a mug."

"His hatred of *all things* knows no bounds."

She rolls her eyes. "I know. I'll clean it in a minute. But first, how exactly did this kiss come about if Chris has such an ironclad rule?"

I turn over again, about to spit out an easy answer, but there isn't one. It came about because we were playing a game. The "if we dated" game.

She nudges me. "C'mon. I can see it in your eyes. Something interesting went down."

"We were just talking, and one of us said something like, 'If we dated we'd do this or that.' And then it kind of spiraled into a kiss?" I say it like a question. Like I'm sorting out how it happened. And perhaps I am.

"Oh, it just spiraled?"

But I know it didn't just happen. We've been building toward it. I shake my head. "No. It was sort of inevitable. We do click. It's crazy. But the thing is, my audience loves the dating segments. Checking my web stats is the biggest rush. It's like a hit of something intoxicating. Every day, it's growing. My views are going up, revenue is up—everything is cooking. I'm starting to make inroads in luring a male audience like Kara, my investor, wants. And really, I shouldn't mess with those efforts. Business is the one reliable thing in my life. Well, besides my dog and my friends."

She offers a smile and squeezes my shoulder.

"That's a pretty solid number of reliable things. But, you know, dating isn't supposed to count."

"Why?" I ask, unsure of her meaning.

"Dating isn't designed to be reliable. It's wild and chaotic and unpredictable. If you like this guy, go for chaos rather than reliability."

The idea is bright and shiny, and I'm the squirrel who wants to snag it. But whatever game Chris and I are playing requires two, and he's stated his position from the start. "He doesn't want to date or get involved. I think he only wanted to kiss. And I wasn't kicking him away for doing that. It was amazing. I can still feel it."

She arches a brow. "He wants to kiss you but not take you out? Ah, hell no."

I nod sadly. "I know, right? But look, I wanted it too. Maybe I just needed to get one fabulous kiss out of my system." I flash her a goofy grin, like that'll get her to agree with my brilliant justification.

"Then don't date him. Just kiss him. And more. Definitely more. Do more than kissing, pretty please?"

"You dirty perv."

"I'm only looking out for your lady parts. I bet they appreciate me being a dirty perv. So I say"—Hayden lowers her voice to a whisper, only after whipping her head around to make sure Lena isn't on the prowl —"kiss him again. And then climb him."

The mere mention of climbing Chris sets my skin on fire, makes my organs positively glow with lust. I bet anyone can see inside me, an X-ray woman, and see I'm zooming toward DEFCON 1 on the scale of readiness.

But there's one little issue.

"I can't make him change his mind," I say.

"No, but you can put yourself out there. Consider it. This dating experiment is led by *you*. It's about what you want. You being ready. You testing the waters. If you're ready for something, try it. And someday, when you least expect it, you'll find someone you'll want to date forever. Your person."

I tear up, my throat catching. She knows what the soft, squishy part of my heart wants again someday.

But right now? It's still too tender.

"Hey. Would you be okay if our girls' night is just girls? No looking for guys or dates or anything?"

"Of course. Whatever you want."

"I don't know that I'm up for it this weekend. I might be *dated out* for the week."

She laughs softly. "And now *dated out* is a thing."

"I suppose it is." I stand, stretch. "I think I'm going to spend the rest of the night with my dog. Thanks for listening."

"Anytime, sweetie," she says as she heads to her kitchen to clean up Chaucer's latest carnage.

I return home, and Ms. Pac-Man is so excited to see me that I give her a kiss on her wet snout. She licks my cheek, a big, sloppy dog kiss, and I love it. "Maybe you're my person."

She whimpers her yes.

She loves me unconditionally, and I love her the same.

I pat the side of my leg, her cue to trot along with me as we head into my bedroom and over to the closet. "Let's look at clothes for tomorrow's shoot, shall we?"

She sits as I survey my wardrobe, watching me, her tail still wagging. I can't resist. I bend down to pet her once more. My dog is the definition of loyal. I don't need anything more.

Except I still want to know what it's like to feel this kind of adored . . . by a person.

21

CHRIS

"Thank you all for attending. We're incredibly grateful for the support of so many business owners and San Francisco icons." The words from the head of the San Francisco Children's Hospital echo across the ballroom as the benefit luncheon draws to a close.

I clap, stand, then say goodbye to our tablemates as I stroll out of the hotel ballroom with Cooper.

"Saw the bit you posted yesterday," he says.

"Stalking me again on social media? You can't get enough of me."

"I know, I know. It's like you're irresistible." He pauses. "Not."

"And yet you watch me."

"Hey, you watch me too," he points out.

"That's different. I have to if I want to watch the Renegades, and I do root for the local team in spite of its ugly-as-sin quarterback. You, however, *choose* to watch me because, admit it, I'm awesome."

He cracks up. "Your modesty knows no bounds.

And to think I was going to wish you luck at staying unentangled."

I furrow my brow. "Why would you wish me luck after seeing the bit I posted?"

"You looked like you brought your girlfriend onto the show."

"Seriously?" This is news to me. "Why the hell would you say that?"

"Have you seen how you two are together?"

"No."

"Then watch a segment, man. You just act like you're, I dunno, a couple."

"We do?"

He claps my shoulder. "It's funny when you can't see what's right in front of you. But yes, it's obvious there's a little something cooking between you two. Bet all your viewers picked up on it. The question now is, what are you going to do about it?"

I sigh heavily.

"Ah, hell. You already did something. You dog."

"It was just a kiss."

He wiggles his eyebrows. "You're into her. You should bring her to karaoke night the next time we all go. Because clearly you have it bad for her."

I shoot him my best skeptical look to avoid the complete and utter truth of his statement. "Please."

"Just admit it. It's obvious. Are you going to ignore it and adhere to your rules? Or are you going to throw a pass under pressure?"

I level with him. "You're in the pocket. The line is coming at you. What do you do?"

He doesn't need time to consider his options. He only has mere seconds—no, split seconds—when he's on the field to make a call. Decisions come quickly to a quarterback. "If I see an opening, I go for it. Always go for it."

I nod, considering his sports wisdom, searching for a way to make it fit my game plan.

Trouble is, he's talking about a high-stakes game played in front of millions every Sunday. He has to go for it.

The rules of my world are different.

At least, I think they are.

* * *

Cooper is right.

The viewers aren't the only ones who see something. Bruce does too. He's all grins when he pokes his head into the studio as we record our segment Saturday morning.

"Vince in San Diego wants to know how to tell the difference between a lie and the truth." I toss the question to the dating expert.

McKenna makes a *yikes* face. "Bring a lie detector with you. Carry it in a murse. It's the only way to be certain."

I laugh but soldier on. "Seriously though. He asks: 'Does a cancellation, a phone call from a friend, or a mention that she has someplace to be after coffee or drinks mean she's not into you?'"

McKenna seems to consider the question, then

answers, "That's the thing about human communication. We don't always know. It's entirely possible she truly has someplace to be. But it's also possible she needs an out. And . . . wait for it . . . it might mean both."

I clasp my skull. "My head is spinning now."

She touches my arm. "I know, right? It's hieroglyphics sometimes, dating. That's why I say your best bet is to be honest and straightforward. Forget games. Just ask her out again, and her answer will make it clear. At the end of the day, if a woman wants to see you, she'll make time for you. And likewise, I'd say that to all women too. Don't make excuses for him. If he wants to date you, he'll show up."

I mime banging a drum. "Truer words. And wait, before I let you go, I have another question I think you're going to love. Don from Tallahassee wants to know if he should wear sneakers, boots, or boat shoes on an upcoming mini-golf date."

McKenna's blue-gold eyes flicker with delight as I tell her more about Don's outfit options for the upcoming date. She settles on hip sneakers and tells him to save the boots for dinner. "After all, it's mini golf you're doing."

I gesture to my feet. I'm wearing casual loafers. "I swear, I only wear flip-flops to play mini golf."

"Well, I hope you have nice feet, then, that look good in flip-flops," she says, a glint in those eyes.

"They're quite handsome nearly naked, thank you very much."

The producer calls cut, and we're done.

Bruce chuckles as he strides over to us. "You two ought to date for real. I'm just saying."

I scoff.

McKenna double scoffs.

He clasps my shoulder. "Ah, don't be such a knucklehead." He turns to McKenna. "I mean, I'm not telling you what to do, Fashion Queen. You're both grown-ups, and you can make these decisions all by yourselves. But you should consider it. Then it'd be really fun for viewers to throw questions at you." He steps back and sweeps his hands out like he's lighting up a marquee. "Picture this: you can answer based on how your dinner-and-a-movie night went. Wouldn't that be funny?" He nudges me. "Funny sells. Funny helps ratings."

I'm speechless. I honestly don't know what to say. I glance at McKenna, and she's quiet too.

"You don't have to smooch or be all kissy face. Just go out and grade each other. A dating report card. Now that's funny!" He holds up his hands in surrender. "Just kidding, just joking. Don't look so serious." He nods toward the door. "And speaking of dinner and a movie, the little lady and I have a date tonight." He sweeps out of the studio, his preposterous idea trailing behind him.

But as I flash back to the way things ended at the taco shop, to Cooper's comments, to the way I feel when I'm with McKenna, maybe it's not so preposterous after all.

When he's gone, McKenna gives me a *what was that all about* look and pushes out a laugh. "He's a little overeager."

Okay, so maybe she thinks it's preposterous.

I slap on a smile. "Yeah, definitely."

See? If there was more cooking, she'd say something, right? Isn't that what she just said on the segment? Or does she want me to say something? But we're not really dating. That's already been established —by both of us.

I do my best to put Bruce's ideas and Cooper's advice out of my head as we make our way out of the studio, discussing how the partnership is going. I share some early numbers, and she tosses some in my direction too. And this—this is clarity. There is no secret language of dating to decipher when we're talking numbers.

Everything adds up to business only.

When we reach the door, she smiles again. "This is going well, isn't it?"

"I couldn't agree more."

Except that's a lie, and I don't need to run a lie detector test on her to see if she can tell.

She knows it. She reads me. She senses it.

And that's when I grab hold of Cooper's advice. That's when I decide Bruce's zany idea isn't so preposterous at all. I'm ready to ask her to cancel the girls' night out and go out with me instead, when her phone trills.

She fishes around in her purse, grabs it, and says, "Aha! It's Handy Andy. I need to take this call. See you next time."

And she walks away.

* * *

The wave crests, and I catch it, riding it beautifully to the shore. The surf is fantastic this afternoon, and I could spend hours in the water. Hours enjoying the crash of the swells, the chance to catch a perfect one, and the challenge of not getting pulled too far under.

But I keep thinking about that damn girls' night out.

And her meeting other guys.

And her coffee class.

And her setups.

And when the next wave comes, I slide into it wrong, and the sea yanks me under forcefully, the ocean a furious beast. Water clogs my throat and swarms my nose, and when I come up, I'm done.

Done with the waves.

Done with the water.

And done with her being out there.

I trudge my way to the shore, load up my board, and get in my car.

I call her.

Texting is for guys who don't know what they want.

22

MCKENNA

I gather my purse and keys as I finish the instructions for Ms. Pac-Man. "Now feel free to enjoy the window view, but don't go crazy if you see Michelangelo."

She tilts her head like she doesn't know who I mean.

"Don't play coy with me. You know who he is," I whisper conspiratorially. "The horny pug."

She growls at the little perv every time he walks by. He tried to hump her once in public.

She lifts her chin higher, asking for a rub. I oblige, scratching her fur. "I know. You're a lady dog. You don't like his cavedog routine."

She whacks her tail against the floor in reply. *Damn straight.*

With my phone stuffed at the bottom of my trendy periwinkle-blue Kate Spade purse—since I don't like when people spend more time on their phones than with the actual company they're keeping—I meet Hayden and catch a Lyft to The Tiki Bar in Fillmore, where we search for Erin and Julia at the venue serving tapas and big, fiery drinks.

The second we find them in a corner booth, Erin shoves a flaming red beverage at me.

I arch a brow. "Vas is das?"

Erin smiles impishly. "Who cares? It's delish."

Julia nods. "It has the bartender seal of approval."

I taste it—it's tangy and sweet with a fiery kick. "Tequila and cherry?"

"Something like that. Sort of like you," Erin says, her big earrings jangling.

"How am I tequila and cherry?"

"You're sweet on the outside, and all sorts of fierce on the inside."

I take another drink, considering. Is that me? Am I sweet but full of fire? If I were, wouldn't I have ignored Andy's call, grabbed Chris by the collar, and said *Take me out tonight*?

But I didn't because I'm only three dates into my new world order, and I still don't know the next steps in the dance. Maybe it's easier to be alone. It's certainly safer. Especially since he's not dating people he works with, and I'm not ready for something serious.

I do my best to push Chris from my mind. The ear-splitting beat of pop tunes overhead does its part.

Erin taps a lacquered red fingernail on the table. "So . . . what's the story? Am I setting you up with the cyclist?"

I shrug. "Can I take a rain check? I'm sort of in a time-out at the moment."

"Already?"

Hayden jumps in. "Hey, dating is hard. Our girl managed three dates in the last two weeks, not to mention all those non-dates with Chris."

Warmth rushes over me at the mention of his name.

Erin motions with her fingers, wiggling them towards her. "Give me the goods. I've been slammed at work the last few days."

As I serve up the deets, we go into a full-on girl huddle. We crowd around the table, tuck in, shoulders hunched. When I'm done with the update, Erin shakes her head in admiration. "I'm impressed."

"At what?" I ask, incredulous.

"At your restraint."

"I should have humped him at the table in the taco bar? Like Michelangelo, the horny pug?"

Erin cracks up, slapping the table. "You could totally go full horny pug on him."

I shake my head, laughing. "You're ridiculous."

"I'm just saying. Michelangelo knows what he wants."

"My dog does not want to be humped by a rando."

"I don't think Chris is a rando."

"You, my friend, are too sex-crazed."

She furrows her brow. "No such thing. I just happen to like sex on the regular. Pete and I have a very healthy sex life, and I think you'd rather enjoy having one too."

"Oh, you think so? Is that it? Like that never occurred to me before."

She knocks back more of her drink then pats my hand, her tone shifting to earnest. "Actually, you have a healthy attitude. You're approaching getting back on the wagon in a thoughtful manner. You've re-entered the dating world with panache, I'd say."

Julia raises a glass. "To panache."

"To our man shield," Erin jokes, as she gestures to our positions and the way we've blockaded the rest of the bar.

Hayden draws a circle in the air with her finger. "There is no man strong enough to penetrate our force field of woman-dom."

"Can you even imagine who'd have the cajones to try to inject himself into this huddle?" I ask, smiling and grateful that I'm enjoying a night out with my best friends. I like, too, that I can do this without needing a man, looking for a man, or hurting over one. "Just let someone try to tell me to cancel this girls' night."

A masculine voice interrupts our reverie.

"I'd tell you to cancel it."

When I look up, Chris is there, staring at me with a hot green-eyed gaze that makes me flush.

All. Over.

23

CHRIS

There are certain rules you don't break as a man.

Don't stare at another dude's junk while he's taking a piss.

Don't carry a murse.

And don't interrupt a girls' night out.

Unless you want to face down a den of lionesses.

But sometimes, you say *screw the rules*. I've battled zombies and artillery-spewing soldiers on a death mission. Hell, I've defeated piranha plants and moon-snakes and beat the game.

I know the way to a woman at a time like this is through her friends, so I address them first. "My apologies for barging in on the sanctity of a girls' night, but I can't let another guy have the chance to go on a date with this fantastic woman before I do."

McKenna clasps her hand to her mouth, and I feel like a king.

I meet her eyes, loving the way they spark with delight, with happiness. "I don't have a clue where this thing between us is going, but I can't stand the thought of you going to a coffee or cheese or wine or sewing or shampooing or how-to-install-a-shower-door class and meeting some other guy. If you and I dated, I'd make sure you wanted to do all that with me and only me. How does that sound to you?"

Her smile is the stuff of dating legends. "I totally want to take a how-to-install-a-shower-door class with you."

When she jumps to her feet, grabs my face, and plants a searing kiss on my lips, I upgrade my status to Rock Star. The kiss short-circuits my brain and fries wires I didn't know were running through my head, charging me up.

McKenna breaks the contact, smiling like that's all she wanted to hear from me, and hell, I'm grinning too.

Her friends cheer us on, and they're beaming too. And it's as if I threw a game-winning touchdown. I'm on top of the world. "I should have done that at the taco shop," I tell her.

"I should have said something too," she says. "And for the record, I never kissed any of those guys. Nothing ever happened with any of them. And I didn't want to meet anyone tonight. After you kissed me, I had no interest in going out and trying to meet a guy at a bar."

My lips curve up in a grin. Pride suffuses me. "Is that so? I ruined you for other kisses?"

"Yes," she says with an over-the-top pout. "And the whole time I was out with the guy from coffee class, I was the worst date ever."

I loop a hand around her waist, yanking her close, glad that I can. "Why's that?"

"I was thinking about you and that epic kiss. And how I wanted to do that with you again. I was officially no fun as a date."

And now I'm simply a happy guy because that's music to my ears. "Good. I'd like to ruin you in other ways though."

A throat clears.

Or maybe a few do.

Feet shuffle and heels click, and three lovely ladies stand and make their excuses. "I can see we aren't needed," says the redhead.

"Glad you came to your senses," the tall brunette says.

"Happy banging," remarks the spiky-haired woman.

I like that hello and goodbye best.

"You guys don't have to go," McKenna says to her pack.

"Yes, we do," the redhead insists.

"Wait. Let me introduce you first."

McKenna makes quick introductions to Julia, Hayden, and Erin, and then they scurry out of The Tiki Bar, and she pulls me down next to her in the booth.

"You sure they're okay with this? Me crashing your night out?"

Her smile is full-wattage. "They're more than okay with it. But how did you find me?"

"I had a tracker put on your ankle," I deadpan.

She glances down at her foot, and then extends one

very sexy leg across my thighs. "Is that so?" she says in a purr.

Damn. She's delicious. I take advantage of this new *thing* between us—I don't know what else to call it—and run my hand over her silky skin. "It's right here," I say, circling my fingers around her ankle, which looks outrageously hot in that black, red-soled shoe. I know fuck-all about fashion, but I know one thing—red-soled shoes are sex in heel form.

"Seriously," she demands. "How did you find me so you could go all caveman and demanding?"

"I think you like the caveman in me." I loop a hand around her waist and haul her in for another kiss, hard on the lips.

When we separate, she rolls her eyes. "Duh. Yeah."

"The other day when you mentioned the girls' night out, you told me you were going to The Tiki Bar. That's how I found you. As to the why, I went surfing this afternoon, got clobbered by the Pacific a couple of times. And then I got pissed that I hadn't manned up and told you I wanted to see you, so I decided to stop playing games. I tried calling, but you didn't answer, and at that point, I was a man on a mission."

She hums sexily. "I'm your mission?"

"Yeah, I think you are," I say, and maybe there's a part of me that's terrified of turbulence again, that's scared of rocking the boat at work, but another part wants to believe we can figure this out. I don't know how, but I like this woman too damn much not to try.

She plays with the ends of my hair, asking, "What's your mission, then?"

I run my fingers down her bare arm, my body electric as I touch her freely. "I think we should date."

"Because Bruce mentioned it? Even though he said he was joking." Her tone is straight-up skeptical.

"It's not a bad idea. But that's not the reason. I want to, and I think you do too." I meet her blue-eyed stare, waiting for her answer, wanting it to match mine.

"I want it too," she agrees softly, a little nervously.

I tuck a finger under her chin. "But listen, I know you just want to have fun. I get that you're not looking for anything more. I respect that. Let's agree that this *thing* will be what it is. We won't push it."

She nods. "We won't define this *thing*."

"We don't let it mess with our heads."

Her smile widens. "We'll be adults. We'll do modern dating on our terms."

"We'll just date. That's all. And we won't expect anything more," I say, because that seems to be the safest way to have her and to maintain the status quo back at the office.

"Nothing serious. No expectations."

I hold up my hands, showing I have nothing to hide. "And if it needs to end, we agree to do it like adults."

"Not like saboteurs."

"Exactly."

"We can be civilized grown-ups. We can fun-date."

"I'll take that," I say. "No-strings-attached dating."

She beams. "I think we just defined it. And defined a new category."

A waitress clicks her way over, parking a hand on her hip. "Can I get you something, sir?"

"Get one of these drinks, Chris," McKenna says, pointing purposefully at the flaming red glass in front of her.

I give her a look like she's crazy. "That's not manly."

"Who cares? It's tasty. Try it," she says, and I lift the glass, but she stops me. "On my lips."

Like I'm going to resist that direct order. I drop a quick kiss to her mouth, aware of the waitress but unable to resist McKenna, who tastes like sugar and fire, and I'm dying for more of this cocktail on her delicious lips. I look to the waitress, answering her at last. "One of these."

When she leaves, McKenna slides a hand along my thigh. "Is this like an officially sanctioned date? Are we truly going to dissect it on your show?"

"Depends on how good it is."

"How good do you think it'll be?"

I squeeze her calf. "I think it'll be great. Call me confident, but I'm already going out on a limb and declaring it worthy of a second date."

She nods crisply. "Then we should do first date stuff."

I hope that involves a lot of nudity. I hope it involves her at my place as soon as humanly possible. "Such as?"

"Music. Talk to me about music."

I laugh because even though I'm dying to get her naked, I'm more than happy to talk music. I go first with the questions. "You like retro tunes. What's your favorite old standard ever?"

"Ever? As in, all-time?"

"Well, yeah. That would be ever."

She looks down. "It's totally cheesy. You'll laugh."

"Try me," I say, eager to get to know her.

She takes a deep breath. "Elvis. 'Can't Help Falling in Love.'"

The look in her eyes tells me that costs her something to admit.

24

MCKENNA

He doesn't say anything for a few seconds, and I tense. Have I scared him? Does he think that means I'm some crazy, clingy girl?

It's just a song, I want to say. Not a declaration.

But instead I wait.

He leans into me and presses his forehead against mine. "That is an awesome song," he says in a soft voice, and I can barely take it anymore, being this close to him. I want to kiss him all night long. The desire to touch him is so overwhelming it's fogging my brain, and all I'm seeing, thinking, feeling is this wish to erase any distance between us.

But then I remember, I *can* do all that now.

We're dating.

Fun-dating is awesome.

I take advantage of it, and I wiggle closer, stealing another kiss, a soft, whispery one that stops my breath, then he blazes a trail of sweet and sexy kisses down to my throat, and it's almost sensory overload the way he ignites me. Forget tingles, forget goosebumps. That's kid stuff compared to this. My body is a comet with Chris. I'm a shooting star from the way he kisses me.

He looks at me, and the expression on his face is one of pride and lust. He knows he's turned me inside out, and all the way on.

We pull apart. I'm gasping. I shake my head, reconnecting thoughts, and somehow I remember what we were talking about. "You like Elvis?"

"Love the King," he says, his voice a sexy rumble, the aftereffects of our kiss. "Love that song."

A sunbeam bursts in my chest. My God, dating someone you like is fantastic. It's like swallowing rainbows. "What about you? What other kind of music do you love?"

"Everything," he says with a sheepish grin.

I shoot him a skeptical look. "Not possible."

"No? You sure? Completely sure it's not possible?"

I shoot him a look. "People say that when they don't want to commit to a type."

He raises a hand like he's taking an oath. "Swear to God. I'm kind of a music whore. I'll listen to rock; jazz; show tunes, thanks to my sister; indie; alt; blues; old standards. I love music in nearly all forms, especially live music. I've actually been to two hundred twenty-seven concerts in my life."

I blink. "Wait. You count concerts?"

He nods proudly.

"You actually count?"

"I have a list on Google Keep of every concert I've ever been to."

"Are you kidding me? That's adorable and super geeky." I clasp his cheek, stroking his five-o'clock stubble.

He leans into my hand. "It's the engineer in me, McKenna. What can I say? I like to keep track of things."

"I so need to get hold of your Google Keep lists." I drop my hand, but I don't disconnect from him. I set it on his leg, loving, no, *adoring* this freedom to touch him. It's exhilarating. Like wearing skyscraper heels with death-defying confidence. Like changing your hair color without testing the look on an app.

"And for that, I'm keeping my desk under lock and key when you come over."

"Hey, where do you live? You never told me."

"It's top secret. But I'll let you in on it." He drops his voice to a clandestine whisper. "Russian Hill. Corner of Polk and Green."

"I love that neighborhood. There is a great little boutique a few blocks north on Polk Street where my sister took me shopping for my last birthday. She got me this bracelet, and then we had cupcakes, and I wear the bracelet with nearly everything because it reminds me how awesome she is. And how much I like having someone who loves cupcakes as much as I do." I show him the delicate rose-gold chain on my wrist.

"Cupcakes are evidence of the existence of God. And your sister sounds fantastic." Chris reaches, gently touching the bracelet. His fingertips graze the top of my hand as he moves along from my finger to my wrist, touching the metal. I am hypnotized by his touch, tugged into an orbit around him. His hands are strong and soft, and they make my skin warm all over, as if I've been lying in the sun, soaking in the delicious rays. He strokes the inside of my wrist briefly, but enough for a tiny whimper to escape my lips as my mind flashes forward to other things he might be able to do with his hands. I press my thighs together so I don't grab him and test my theories in public.

But in private, later? I'll be all over that.

"You know, McKenna," he says, rubbing his thumb and forefinger along the rose-gold. "I like the way you dress. I noticed that about you the first time we met."

"You did?" This delights me immeasurably.

"That time at the electronics store, the first thing I noticed was how hot you were." He slides his hands up my arm, my hungry skin drinking in the wondrous sensation of his touch. "The second thing I noticed was you were funny. The third was that you were interesting. And the fourth thing I noticed was you had on this sexy outfit that kind of accentuated all the places I wanted to touch."

I smile. Or maybe I beam, lit from head to toe. Because I don't know which of those four things I like better—hot, funny, interesting, or stylish enough to be sexy. I like them all for different reasons, but I have to say he saved the best for last. He likes my style. He likes what makes me *me*, and that's all I need to fall totally under his spell, body and heart.

"No one has ever said that to me," I say as I linger on his eyes for a moment, his Hawaii eyes pools of green that stare intensely. He's looking at me like he wants to strip me bare, and I desperately want that.

God, I hope fun-dating includes hot banging.

The waitress brings his drink. He takes a swallow, throws down some bills, and says, "Now, if memory serves, you once said you could take me down in *Q*bert*."

I grin. "I did, didn't I?"

"Are you still up for it?"

"Are you inviting me over?" I pray he says yes. Possibly even make offerings to the gods of banging.

"I believe I am."

There is a goddess!

We are so civilized in the Lyft, I want to give us a medal. We hold hands in the back seat and exchange naughty looks. I touch his arm. He glides his fingers along my legs.

Okay, fine. We aren't Goody Two-Shoes. He does try to slip that hand a little farther north.

But he catches himself, jerking his hand out of my skirt and setting it primly on my knee as the driver stops at a red light on Van Ness.

"I deserve a gold star for restraint, don't you think?" He wiggles his eyebrows.

"Definitely. Do you have any stickers at your house? Maybe in that drawer next to your concert list?"

"Oh, mock me, why don't you, for my analytical brain?"

I lean in closer and whisper in his ear, "It's not your analytical brain I want tonight. It's the dirty one."

He shakes his head in appreciation. "You are on fire. And I'm going to have a field day with you."

He dips his head to my neck and sucks on my skin, nipping me. I manage not to groan audibly, which I think is silver-star worthy.

When the car arrives and we get out, the restraint time ends, but not in a frenzy.

As soon as we reach the steps to his home, a classic San Francisco Victorian building, he closes his fingers over mine, gripping my hand in his. Within seconds, I'm in his arms, and we're wrapped up in each other. His lips sweep mine, and I press my hands against his chest, and he does have the most fantastic body. He's toned everywhere, strong everywhere, and I'm dying to get my hands up his shirt and feel his bare chest and his abs.

He twines his fingers through my hair, and the way he holds me, both tender and full of want at the same time, makes me start to believe in possibilities. Start to believe I can try again, and that it'll be worth it.

Dangerous thoughts though. I vacuum them up. They don't belong in this brand-new category of no-strings-attached dating.

I focus on the physical. His lips are soft, so unbearably soft, and I can't stop kissing him. He has the faintest taste of cherry and tequila on his lips, and it drives me wild. Or maybe he's driving me wild as he tugs me against him, the press of his body revealing his want, his desire for me. He's so hard, so aroused, and

I'm not kidding when I say it thrills me to the marrow of my bones.

There's no space between us, and I don't want there to be space between us. I grab his T-shirt, my fingers curled tightly around the fabric.

He breaks the kiss, breathing hard, his voice low and smoky. "Get inside."

I flash him my naughtiest smile. "I could say the same thing to you."

25

MCKENNA

He unlocks the main door, and we walk up two flights of stairs. As we round the stairwell, his hands are on my waist, and he's telling me all the things he wants to do to me.

Undress you now.

Strip you naked.

Kiss you everywhere.

Taste you, touch you, feel you.

Make you come again and again and again.

And on that note, I'm officially liquefied. "You know, it's not going to take me long when you talk like that."

"Good. That's the goal. And then I'll do it one more time." He opens the door to his place, and it's spacious, with a wide living room that stretches the whole length of the building, it seems. I spot a few arcade games off in the corner, including *Q*bert*, and for a moment I pretend I'm a zombie, drawn to it. Chris circles his hands around my waist, picks me up, and carries me.

He turns me around, setting my butt on the console.

His eyes blaze with wicked intent. "Want to play *Q*bert* a whole new way?"

"Yes," I answer breathlessly. It is the only answer.

I glance down at my short black skirt, and he pushes it higher, practically growling when he gets the first peek at white lace. He bends lower, kissing the inside of my thighs, softly trailing his tongue from my knee all the way up, then darting over to the other leg.

"You taste like sugar," he murmurs.

"I dusted myself in it before I went out tonight."

He laughs lightly then presses a hot kiss to the lace, and I can't make any more jokes. I moan.

It feels glorious to be kissed like this.

He tugs off my underwear and spreads my legs. "Look at you. All hot and wet."

He bends lower and licks my thigh, and the sound I make is obscene. I sound like an animal, and I feel like one too.

He groans his approval. "I like that. Keep that up all you want."

I moan his name as he teases me. He nibbles lightly on my thigh as his strong hands spread me wider. I accidentally bump the start button, and even though he hasn't put a quarter in the game, the theme music from *Q*bert* begins. I laugh, and so does he, but then my laugh turns into a long, low moan at the first flick of his tongue on me. I've entered an altered state, buzzing with bliss, crackling with heat. He's magnificent, his tongue divine as he traces delirious lines up and down my center, making me whimper.

My noises seem to drive him. Each sound that

tumbles from my lips makes him groan too. We become a feedback loop of wanting and giving, of taking and consuming, as I burn hotter with every single touch. I'm in heaven. I grip the edge of the game console as he devours me with his mouth, somehow both soft and hungry in the fevered slide of his lips.

His hands slink under my thighs, and he lifts my legs onto his shoulders, draping them over his back. I'm vaguely aware that I'm so completely vulnerable, giving myself to him, but it feels so right. I let go completely, panting as I say his name and tell him how good it feels.

He brings me to the edge of bliss and shatters me with an orgasm that's as endless as it is intense. I let go of the side of the game and grab his hair, holding on to him as I come hard, seeing stars, seeing distant galaxies.

When my vision clears, I find him standing and staring at me with those dreamy eyes that reflect everything I want. I kiss him, tasting myself on his lips, tasting what he just did to me. "That was out of this world. You know how to go down on a girl."

He kisses my forehead. "That's because I can't get enough of you. And now I want all of you."

"Have me."

He tugs me off the game and carries me to his bedroom where he strips me in seconds flat.

I'm a speed racer myself as I yank off his shirt, stopping to savor the sight of his chest. My fingers itch to finally touch him, and I trace the hard lines everywhere, from his beautifully defined pecs, down across each hard ab to the edge of the promised land.

As he unzips his jeans and shoves them off, my busy hands make their way down to his boxer briefs. I cup his erection, thrilling at the feel of him through the fabric. He grabs my hand, stroking my palm against his hard length.

"You drive me crazy. You have since I met you," he rasps.

"Let's drive each other crazy." I pluck at the waistband of his briefs. "And to do that, I'm going to need to remove these."

"Be my guest," he says as I strip off his underwear.

He's naked in front of me, and I can't get enough. My eyes roam up and down his body, admiring his long legs, his toned arms, the shape and tightness of his body. It's like he's been carved by the waves he rides, and my mouth waters.

Especially as I touch his hard, hot length.

He feels so heavy in my hand, thick with wanting, pulsing against my palm. It's intoxicating to know I've done this to him. That we do this to each other.

"You're perfect," I whisper reverently, because his body ought to be worshipped.

"You are," he says, then we tumble onto the bed while he reaches for a condom on the nightstand.

He rolls it on. He's beautiful, every inch of him, and he's so sexy as he prepares to enter me. I place my hands on his shoulders, but then he shifts so he's on his back. He moves me on top of him.

"Let me watch you ride me," he murmurs.

"I might watch you too."

"Feel free." He grins and brushes a strand of hair away from my cheek, his hands traveling to my hips as he positions me over his length.

I lower myself onto him, gasping when he slides inside. I draw a sharp intake of breath, close my eyes, and let the feeling of him filling me up take over my mind and body. I open my eyes again and look down at him. His expression is tense, his jaw tight.

"That feels so fucking good," he says.

A wave of lust crashes over me, knowing he wants me the way I want him. This is the dating dream. To meet someone you connect with in every way.

I move slowly at first, taking my time, rising up and down. I savor the feel of him inside me, stretching me. It's a deliciously lazy kind of rhythm, in and out, long and leisurely strokes as I swivel my hips, riding him.

He groans as I move, as I take him in deep. Gritting his teeth, he grunts like he needs more.

"Fuck me," I whisper.

Then we're not so leisurely. He picks up the pace, thrusting, pushing, driving deeper. He's hitting me in all the right spots, and my mind goes hazy, my body burns hot.

Sparks fly over my skin, racing through my veins. I close my eyes, because reality is too intense right now to have to see it. I want to feel, only to feel. I lean down to kiss him, and he draws me against him, my breasts pressing into his chest, his hands grabbing my ass.

Being this close to him trips a switch in me. Pleasure tightens and intensifies, a warning signal. "I have to tell you something," I whisper.

"Tell me."

"I think I'm going to come again. Really soon. Can you go a little harder? Faster?"

A groan takes over him as he thrusts harder, pumps up into me. "I can fuck you however you want. I can fuck you fast and dirty."

"Yes." Pleasure zips down my spine as he fucks up into me, rocking his hips, driving me wild. Sending me racing to the edge.

My belly tightens. It coils, and I'm tipped over, past the point of no return, as another orgasm washes over me.

I shudder, crying out in pleasure and then in surprise when he pulls out, flips me to my back, and drives into me again. He hikes up my thigh, going deeper and chasing his own release.

Digging my nails into his back, I urge him on. "I want to feel you come," I say, growly and desperate for his release.

There's something incredibly freeing about sex with Chris.

It's wild and open and honest.

And I want his pleasure as much as I want my own.

The sounds he makes are carnal and filthy. He's nothing but a string of grunts and curse words, and I love it. I absolutely love his abandon. And the filthiest word of all is *yes*. That's all he says—a long, raw, brutal *yes*—as he comes hard and deep inside me.

A minute later, after we stop panting like we've run

a race, he tosses the condom, returns to my side, and runs his fingers down my stomach. "So, you still want to play my *Q*bert*?"

I laugh out loud, not expecting those words but loving how perfect they actually are. "Only if you think I'll score as well as I did just now."

"There's only one way to find out."

26

CHRIS

This might be my new favorite sight ever.

The beautiful naked woman playing a game I built.

Wait. Let me revise that.

The beautiful naked woman who called out my name, who's completely awesome, and who's as into me as I'm into her playing a game I built.

Yes, that's what makes the sight fantastic.

Right now, as I relax on the couch, I'm enjoying the view a helluva lot. Her ass is spectacular, all heart-shaped and soft where it needs to be and firm where it ought to be, and so tempting.

As if she's worshipping the console, she runs a hand across the control panel, stroking the joystick against her palm. Her fingers trace the name in its big balloon-y print. Resting her cheek against the screen, she sighs contentedly.

"You sure you don't want me to leave you alone with it?" I tease.

"Yes, please. I need several moments," she says then

jerks her head up, clearly distracted by the *Galaga* machine to the right and the *Donkey Kong* next to that.

"My God, you have your own arcade, Chris."

I park my hands behind my head. "Would you be impressed if I told you I built them all myself?"

Her eyes pop. "You built all these arcade games?"

"You make it sound like I made a time machine out of a DeLorean. It wasn't that hard."

"Wasn't that hard?" she parrots back. "How do you *make* an arcade game?"

"I dusted off a computer, found some source code from a non-profit development project that preserves old arcade games, tweaked it up a bit, and then built the cabinet."

"This is amazing. You can fix and you can build. You have some serious *skills*."

"That is true. I've already introduced you to some of my finest ones tonight. Now get playing, woman, so I can give you another orgasm."

A wicked smile stretches across her gorgeous face. "This is the first time I've ever played it wanting to get killed, but with you dangling that kind of prize ..."

"The way I see it is you win either way—you get the high score or you score again."

"That's definitely what I call a win/win." She winks, spins back around, feeds the machine a quarter from a stack on the console, and goes to town, jamming on the joystick.

Gamer that she is, she doesn't just roll over. She plays hard, and it's hot as hell watching her.

So hot that by the time she finally plummets off the

side of the pyramid, I'm good and ready for another round in bed, and she is too.

This time, we're slower. We take our time, kissing as we go, exploring each other. She's warm and pliant, and as she lifts her knees higher and pulls me in deeper, it feels like she's giving herself to me. It feels like I could do this with her for many, many nights. Nights I don't want to end.

After we finish, I ask her to stay over.

"I was hoping you'd extend an invitation," she says, then hums a happy sound.

She stretches out under the sheets, arranging herself for sleep, and I bring her against me, sighing at the feel of her warm skin against mine. She curls against me as moonlight sneaks through the blinds, casting a silver glow over her arms and shoulders.

"I like you, Chris," she says, her voice sleepy.

I kiss the back of her neck. "I like you too. A lot."

"I'm glad you made me your mission tonight."

"I'm going to make you my mission on our next date too."

"I like the sound of that."

I do too.

I like the sound of all of this.

As she falls asleep, I'm struck with the realization that we're quickly zooming past no-strings-attached dating.

And I don't seem to mind the strings.

* * *

The preliminary numbers are in. The segments are a hit. Viewers love the chemistry between McKenna and me. And more than that—they love her.

That's what Bruce tells us the next time we're in the studio, ready to shoot again.

"They're going to want you to do a show all by yourself," I tell her.

She pokes my chest. "Don't be silly. They'll want me to take over for you."

"You know, Needle Arms, she has a darn good idea," Bruce says with a glint in his eyes.

"I'm cool with that. I can surf all day and eat my avocado toast with smashed beets anytime I want."

He cringes. "Ah, why do you do this to me? I'm going to have to eat some bacon to make up for hearing about your health food."

McKenna shoots me a curious look. "I take it he doesn't know about your penchant for orgasmic ketchup on your succulent fries?"

Bruce's eyes widen. "You're secretly eating my kind of food?"

I press a finger to my lips. "Shh. Don't tell my boss."

Bruce stage-whispers, "He already knows." In his normal voice, he tells us the first question from viewers.

I gulp.

McKenna blushes.

The question hits close to home.

"You good with that?" Bruce inquires.

I meet McKenna's eyes. She nods her assent.

"Yes," I tell him.

A little later, we record.

"And on today's What to Do on a Date segment, Denny from St. Louis wants to know: When is it a good idea to sleep together on the first date?"

The faint blush of pink on her cheeks delights me, and feels like both a secret and a statement. She looks to the camera as she answers the question we both have recent firsthand experience with. "I would say it's a good idea if you're two adults who communicate clearly about expectations. That's the key—to talk. To be clear with each other." She turns to me. "Don't you think, Chris?"

I rein in the grin, the ridiculous, oversized one threatening to occupy all the square footage of my face. "I do, McKenna. There's never a guarantee as to what happens next, but as long as you can be straight from the get-go, that's the best path. So each person knows the score."

"But remember, too, sometimes sex on the first date can be a terrible idea. And sometimes it can be a great idea. The difference usually lies not in the act itself, but in the talking about it beforehand." Once more, she looks my way, a naughty twinkle in her blue eyes. "And if the sex is good, definitely do it again with a second date."

I shrug happily, pointing at her. "That's what she said."

And that's what we plan to do later that night. But first, we play mini golf. Per her advice, I wear flip-flops.

She wiggles her butt as she preps to swing the club at a windmill.

"Your shoes are fantastic," I say, just as she lets loose.

Her shot is all kinds of wrong. She shoots me a withering glare. "You're trying to knock me off my game."

I shrug. "You'd expect nothing less of me."

She grumbles, narrowing her eyes. "I'm going to crush you, Chris McCormick."

"Be my guest," I say as she lines up again. "Also, those jeans look great on you."

I'm the recipient of another sharp stare as she saunters over to me. "You are not playing fair. Complimenting my clothes to try to get me to balk."

"And it's working."

She splays a hand across my stomach, dragging her fingertips in a way that revs my engine. "Two can play at that game."

I smile and haul her against me for a kiss. I'm intoxicated by her taste, buzzed on her, and having a great time. I flash back to earlier, what we both said in the studio. *The key is to talk.* That's been the refrain of all our segments—be honest, be open, tell the truth.

When I break the kiss, I cup her cheek. "I'm glad you were amenable to fun-dating."

"Me too."

"We should keep doing it."

"You angling for a third date already?"

I smile. "Hell yeah."

She dances her fingers up my chest. "Good. Because I want a third one too."

The rest of the game, I'm a good boy. I don't try to

distract her with compliments or too many kisses. Instead, we talk as we go, chatting about her dog, and she tells me how much she's relied on the pooch. I tell her about my friendship with Cooper. How we rib each other constantly, but how we're also straight shooters when we need to be. She shares a few stories about her sister and their rabid love of cupcakes. I tell her about Jill, and how hard she's worked for her shot on a Broadway stage.

When we're done, I've won the game.

But it feels like we've both won something else.

A normal, terrific, fantastic date, and neither one of us needed to order a lobster to get some good action.

Because that's what we have when we go home to her house. I say hi to her dog, then I get her clothes off in seconds flat, and I send her soaring.

As she wraps her arms around me, I can feel my trust issues slipping out the door.

Good riddance. I won't miss them.

27

MCKENNA

"Here's one of my favorite parts of dating. I get to do what I like best—devote my mental energy to assembling cute outfit combos," I say to the phone camera, then model the newest ensemble I'm wearing for tonight's date with Chris: a swingy little skirt from ModCloth, silver Rag & Bone ankle boots, and a sapphire-blue top I snagged from the best place of all— Target. "Here's the key—don't forget that picking an outfit for the third date with a guy you really like is all about *you*. Sound selfish? Hardly. Wear what makes you feel pretty. Wear what makes you feel good about yourself. That's what makes a great date outfit."

I click end then shoot another video, this one with tips for guys (*Don't wear what makes you feel pretty, wear what you think she'll like*). When I'm done, I head to my bedroom, take off the clothes, and leave them on my bed. I pull on a soft T-shirt and jeans and return to my living room, where Andy works diligently from my couch, Ms. Pac-Man commandeering the spot next to him, her snout resting on his leg.

He pets her as he works. "I'm checking out the numbers. Looks like you're definitely seeing an uptick in dudes, according to the site demographics," he says, glancing up from his screen.

"Excellent. Good to see the strategy is working. Would you mind sending that report to Kara at Redwood? I updated her the other day, but she can't get enough of numbers going in the right direction, especially when it comes to men. That was one of the key goals for her investment."

I settle in at my desk, editing the videos for posting, humming an Elvis tune under my breath as I type. Out of the corner of my eye, I see Andy smirking.

"Spill. What's that little grin all about?" I stare at him over the screen of my laptop.

"Oh, I was just curious how well *your* strategy is working."

My brow knits with confusion. "I thought you just said it was working."

He shakes his head slowly. "No, the strategy where you don't fall for the guy you're dating."

"What are you talking about?" I say, choosing to play dumb because it's easier than facing the stark truth.

He rolls his eyes. "Seriously, girlfriend," he says, adopting some over-the-top sass.

"Seriously, guy-friend," I mimic.

"McKenna, you just sat there humming 'Can't Help Falling in Love' as you worked."

I pretend to be outraged. "I did not."

He slices a hand through the air. "You did. Fess up. You're falling for this guy in a major way."

I huff, shrugging. "I like him. A lot. What's so wrong with that?"

"Nothing is wrong with it. If it's what you want. I'm just making sure you're ready. You went into this dating project with a clear goal—to have fun again."

"And it is fun," I interrupt.

"Yes, dating is fun," Andy says diplomatically as he pushes a shock of hair from his forehead. "Until feelings get involved."

"It's not fun then?"

"It can be. But it shifts. It becomes real."

"Is that why you prefer hookups?"

He nods and gives a closed-mouth smile that strikes me as a little sad. "I'm no good at relationships. So I keep everything at a distance. But that's my MO, and it has been for a while. You're wired differently. You're wired for relationships, and I'm pretty sure that's what's happening with this guy. You're falling into a relationship."

I glance away as if I've been caught. "I don't think that's the case."

"You truly don't?"

I steel myself, meeting his gaze again. "That would make me foolish. I'm not foolish. I'm practical. Chris and I made a deal. Just fun-dating. No-strings-attached dating. That means we're not going to fall into a relationship."

"Fine. Just be careful. Watch your heart. I don't want to see it get bruised again."

I cover the organ in question. "Don't worry. I've got this baby on lockdown."

He barks a laugh, the kind that says he doesn't quite believe me. "Keep the key in a place only you can find. Okay?"

"I promise."

A little later, I tell him I'm going to shower before my date.

Looking at his watch, he says, "It's only five."

"Well, sometimes a girl likes to take her time getting ready for her guy."

He closes his laptop, smirking. "*Her guy.*" As he speaks, he sketches air quotes. "Good luck on your 'fun date.'"

"It'll be fun. It's just a date. That's all."

But as he leaves, I'm not so sure that's true any longer.

Or that I want it to be.

* * *

I spend more time than usual getting ready. I shave my legs and spread the softest strawberry lotion into my skin, thinking of how it would feel if Chris's hands were the ones on my legs right now.

I tremble, picturing him kissing his way up my body. I blow out my hair, imagining his fingers twined through it.

I do my makeup as I listen to all my favorite songs,

like "I've Got a Crush on You" and "Fly Me to the Moon." It's as if I'm living in the lyrics, wrapped up in the hope they promise. I find myself swaying to the words as I swipe on my blush, imagining Chris behind me, his arms around my waist as he peppers kisses on my neck and we lose ourselves to the music.

I dress in the outfit I modeled today on my video. An outfit that makes me feel pretty. Desired. Wanted.

And something more. Something new. Something I can't quite place, so I stop trying.

I kiss my dog goodbye and head to a comedy club, where we're checking out some up-and-coming comedians.

When I arrive, I see Chris waiting outside, wearing earbuds and lip-synching.

Nerves slam into me. All that warm fuzziness of my alone time flies away, and now I'm faced with the *how much am I feeling* dilemma. And can I handle it?

But before I have time to decipher the growth of my feelings, he spots me, smiles, and takes out the earphones.

"Rockabilly? Blues? Jazz?" I ask.

His lips tip up in a smile as he shakes his head. "A preview of my sister's cast album recording for *Crash the Moon*. She sent me a cut of one of her songs."

I make grabby hands. "Gimme."

"Only if you promise to keep it top secret."

"Swear on my love of Dior knockoffs I won't say a word," I say, crossing my heart over my Target top.

"In that case . . ." He hands me the earbuds, and I

listen, my eyes widening as my ears fall in love with each gorgeous verse.

When the song is over, I bounce on the toes of my ankle boots. "It's like listening to a Pink Floyd bootleg in the seventies. At least, I think that's what it's like. I was never a Pink Floyd fan. But my dad is. He had all these bootleg albums."

Chris smiles. "I'm going to pretend you didn't say you're not a Pink Floyd fan."

"What? Is that a crime? Their music is too slow and druggy for me."

"Pink Floyd is awesome. Every single song. I love Pink Floyd."

"But see, you love everything. So based on that, it'll never be fair for me to dislike anything, then."

He laughs and loops an arm around me, guiding me into the club. "You're a hoot. You know that, right?"

"I'm going to assume a hoot is the highest of compliments," I say, raising my chin haughtily as we sit at a small table near the front.

He captures my jaw in his hand. "Hey." His tone has shifted. It's softer, but more urgent. "Is everything okay?" he asks intently.

I nod.

He dips his face to mine, capturing my lips in a chaste kiss that still manages to lick the flames inside me. "I needed to kiss you. I didn't get to on the street."

I sigh against his mouth. "How do you do that?"

"Do what?"

"Kiss me like that?"

He slides his thumb along my jaw. "Like it's all I want to do?"

My heart executes a back handspring in my chest. Holy shit. I didn't know my heart knew that move. It nailed the landing too. "Yeah. Just like that," I say with a dopey grin.

"Because kissing you *is* all I want to do. I can't get enough." He drops his mouth to mine and gives me a brand-new kind of kiss.

It's the kind that makes the world fall away, that leaves me powerless to resist, helpless to do anything but be consumed by it. Nothing else matters, and the kiss is all there is and all I'll ever want.

Until it becomes more than a kiss. It becomes imbued with emotions.

"I need to tell you something," I whisper when we break apart, feeling emboldened now.

"It better be good."

I touch his cheek, tracing his stubble. "You're getting under my skin. I can't stop thinking about you. Can't stop wanting to see you."

The smile that spreads on his face is vulnerable and wildly happy too. "In that case, you should keep seeing me. Because I can't get you out of my head either. Or my heart."

I'm giddy, bubbling inside. "This is crazy, don't you think? How this happened with us?"

He sighs happily. "I do think it's crazy, but I also don't. Mostly, I know I don't want it to stop."

We don't say a word about trust issues. We don't dissect the ones we both have. Maybe that time has passed. Or maybe we're figuring out what matters more. Because the biggest issue I have right now is with myself. It's believing in my own feelings. Trusting my heart. That's why Andy's assessment scared me. That's why I tried to pretend this wasn't happening.

But this *is* happening. I can't deny the truth of my feelings when I'm with Chris. My heart would slap me and call me a liar.

So I don't even try to ignore the way my toes curl and my body melts and my soul seems to sing when I'm with him.

"Don't stop," I whisper.

He leans in for another kiss, and we continue stealing little kisses from each other all throughout the show. We laugh at the funny bits and clap at the end of each act, and we tip the waitress on the way out.

On the street, Chris yanks me close once again. As if he can't stop touching me. "By the way, you look beautiful tonight. Sorry I didn't tell you earlier."

"I'll gladly accept the compliment now. Even though I suspect you're only saying it to get a blow job."

He blinks, jerking away. "What?" His tone is high-pitched. "Where did that come from?"

I smile like a little vixen. "Don't think I haven't noticed that you haven't given me the chance to go down on you yet, which is highly unfair of you. But I plan on rectifying that tonight."

He drags a hand through his hair, breathes a sigh of relief, then orders a Lyft, stat. "Rectify me all night long," he says as we get in the car.

* * *

At his house, I make quick work of his jeans, unzipping them as he tugs off his T-shirt. I push him to the couch, and he falls easily, grinning as he flops down.

"Let the great rectifying begin," he declares.

"And so it shall." I take his erection in my hand, wrapping my palm around his length. He groans, a long, low, insanely sexy rumble.

"I've been picturing this for a while." I stroke up, squeezing the tip.

"What took you so long, woman?"

I narrow my eyes. "It's only our third date."

"Like I said, what took so long?"

"You were always busy pleasuring me. You didn't give me a chance."

"Now's your chance."

"And I'm taking it. Stop talking because it makes me talk back, and when I'm talking, I can't suck your dick."

He purses his lips like they're glued shut. But his eyes are wide open, his gaze intense as he watches me drop my lips to him, kissing the head.

He twitches, his hips jerking up.

And that's a very nice start.

I lick him, then draw him in deeper, every move rewarded by a dirty groan, a hoarse *yeah*, a feral grunt. The noises he makes are music to my ears, and I take him in all the way, savoring the taste of him in my mouth.

He breathes out hard, cursing his appreciation. "I've thought about your lips on me," he says as he

runs a fingertip against my mouth. "These lips of yours
. . ."

He doesn't finish the thought as I give him a tight,
hard suck. I flick my tongue along his length as I move
up, down, up, down, my fast rhythm punctuated by his
growls and groans, by the arch of his hips, by the way
his hands curl around my head. His fingers thread
through my hair, and he drops his head back against
the cushions as if this is all too much.

Too good.

I love the way he's relinquishing himself to pleasure. His desire drives me on. His sounds make me go
faster, take him deeper, and lavish attention on him till
he jerks me away unexpectedly, his voice strangled.
"You keep doing that, and I'll come."

"That's the point."

His hand tightens in my hair. "I need to be inside
you. Now."

His intensity sends me into stratospheric pleasure,
and I feel as if I could come without even being
touched, just from how he sounds. How he needs me.

I've never felt this way before.

Never been so turned on by pleasuring a man.

I'm melting with lust for him. "I need you too."

In seconds—nanoseconds, maybe—he's taken my
skirt off, and he doesn't even bother with my top or my
boots. He just slides me under him on the couch,
flailing around for a condom.

I grab his hand, stopping him. "I'm on birth control,
and I'm clean."

"Me too."

That's all we say. In an instant, he's inside me, and I nearly cry from the pleasure. From the sheer bliss of him filling me completely.

He rocks into me, and there's a new urgency, a desperation, even. It's like we're chasing something. Something new, something scary, but something beautiful too.

There's another level in this game. A bonus. An Easter egg. And it's one I didn't see coming.

Maybe one I didn't want to see coming.

But when he swivels his hips and drives deeper into me, all I see are stars. Bright sparks burst behind my eyes as I soar on a wave of white-hot pleasure. It stretches, reaches, flies until I tumble, toppling over the edge with him right beside me, holding my hand as we jump.

Neither one of us says anything for a while. We just breathe, hard and loud.

He takes my hand, pulls me up, and takes me to his bathroom, turning on the shower. He makes the water as hot as any human can stand, then he soaps up his hands and slides them over me, soft and tender.

Neither one of us has said a word.

Speechless is such a strange state for us.

He breaks the silence, cupping my cheek. "How are we doing?"

I swallow nervously. "We?"

He nods, gesturing from him to me. "With this *thing*? This fun-dating thing?"

I rise up on tiptoes, dust my lips over his, and whisper, "I think it's more than fun."

"It's so much more than fun."

That's all either one of us says. But it feels like enough to change the game. My heart stutters, and there's a part of me who wants to run home, jump in bed, and snuggle with my dog in a place where my heart is safe and can never be hurt again.

Because this place here with him is no longer a safe zone. It's teeming with risks I didn't expect to face.

I kiss him once more to blot out the whispers of past disappointments, past hurts, the murmurs of doubt.

28

CHRIS

It's Monday morning, which means meeting with the boss man. I bring him coffee this time, steam rising from the cup in a tantalizing plume. Plunking it down on his desk, I give him an *I did good* look.

He nods his approval.

"But wait. There's more." I dip my hand into the paper bag and grab a yogurt cup with chia seeds and potent probiotics.

He raises his hands to block my approach, averting his face like a vampire I'd offered garlic toast to. "What are you trying to do to me?"

"What? I thought you liked probiotics?"

"Do you even know what a probiotic is?"

I shrug as I plop down in the chair. "I do, and they're good for you."

He shakes his head, correcting, "Good for you till they find out they're bad for you."

"Oh, I forgot. You're on the nothing-good-for-you diet."

"If they discovered that coffee was good for you, would you stop drinking it until they changed their minds?"

"Not funny, kid. But since they haven't . . ." He takes the coffee and drinks some, with a satisfied smack and a sigh afterward. "Now, this is good. And if it's harvested by humanely raised local bear cubs, I don't want to know."

"It's from Dunkin."

"Now you're talking. And now, let's talk." Sliding on his reading glasses, he riffles through some papers on his desk. "Emails."

I cringe. "You printed out emails."

"Please. No, my assistant did."

"Dude, you know that's a waste of paper?"

"How else can I read 'em?"

"On your phone, like everyone else. Or, hey, even a computer. How about that?"

"When you're my age, you lose interest in reading everything on a screen. Now, first of all, Zander Kendrick's manager says he'll be calling you today to set up the interview."

I strum a triumphant power chord on my air guitar. "Excellent."

"Good things are cooking indeed. Also, viewers love the segments with McKenna. And . . ." He stops, peers over his glasses. "You two did take my advice, didn't you?"

We haven't dissected our dates on the show as he'd suggested. But the chemistry is there, and I don't try to deny it. "I think that's fair to say."

He grins like a sly dog. "I had a feeling. It makes for that little extra spark. But it makes me a little nervous, admittedly, given the past."

My muscles tighten. The last thing I want is for the boss to be uneasy. "It's not the same."

"I know. I can tell. And the viewers can too. This is different. Just listen."

As I eat the yogurt, he proceeds to read a sampling of the emails, and it's like I'm being sprinkled with gold dust. I couldn't be happier that the new concept has gone over so well.

After we tackle a few more items, he hands me the stack of papers. "Be sure to share the viewer comments with your lovely lady. And don't forget—always tell her how special she is to you."

"Thanks, Bruce," I say, appreciating the rare moment of candor and honest advice from the guy.

"She's a good one. So are you. And listen, I know you beat yourself up about the other one. But you're right—this isn't the same. Not one bit. Carly wasn't a happy person. She took it out on you."

I'm surprised he's so aware of the details, since I never discussed Carly with him. But then, Bruce doesn't miss much. He might be old-school, he might print his emails, he might cringe at my occasionally hipster ways, but he's sharp and whip-smart at his job. He sees everything and steps in when he needs to.

"Thanks. I think I needed to hear that."

I head to my office, noodling on what he said. The assurance was good to hear, but as I sink down in my leather chair and flip through the emails, I'm also aware that I've had to reach the same conclusion, and to do so on my own terms.

Carly is the past. She's not my present, and she's not my future. I can't let whatever mistakes she or I made then dictate how I live my life now.

And how I love.

I can't give the past that power.

And I won't.

That knowledge fills me with a newfound certainty as I read through a few more emails.

Most of them make me smile.

But then I come across one that's not quite so smiley face.

Chris:
Your new segment sux. It's boring AF and obvious you just put your GF on the show to get into her pants. Go back to game talk. Not the dating game.
David

Ouch.

That hurts.

I set the page down and shift my gaze to the wall and a framed photo of a surfer gloriously riding through the barrel of a fifty-footer. The waves curl over him majestically, threatening to take him under if he doesn't ride it just so.

Just right.

Just like he knows how.

Because this guy knows balance.

I take the paper, crumple it up, and toss David's note into the recycling bin. I'm sure it was an oversight that Bruce's assistant printed this email for me.

Just as I'm sure that it doesn't bother me.

A couple weeks ago—hell, a few days ago—it would have gnawed away at my confidence, made me wonder if I was giving my all to *Geeking Out*, or if I was getting distracted by a girl.

Now?

I want the perfect girl more than I want a perfect show.

The show is good enough. Hell, it's great most of the time. It doesn't have to be perfect, and it doesn't have to be everything to everyone.

I'm doing my best, and that's all I can do.

As I turn to my computer to work on the lineup for the next episode, my phone buzzes on my desk.

Grabbing it, I find a message from my buddy.

Cooper: Yo. Karaoke tonight with the crew. You still in? You bringing your new woman?

Chris: I'm down. Let me check with her.

Cooper: Ah, so you do admit you're into her.

Chris: Yeah, the cat's out of the bag on that.

Cooper: I knew it. I'm always right.

Chris: If you're always right, tell me you'll win next weekend in Baltimore.

Cooper: I'll own Baltimore. Also, I'll see your skinny ass tonight. I'm thinking Foreigner's "Feels Like the First Time" ought to bring the crowd home.

Chris: You should have been on a Broadway stage. You're such a performer.

Cooper: I believe you mean in a stadium. Since I was clearly a rocker in my other life.

Chris: Such an active imagination too.

I'm about to text McKenna when I decide I'd rather hear her voice.

She answers on the first ring. "Hey! What are you up to?"

Like the wave just crested, I slide into the barrel, going for it. "I got this note from a viewer. It was all about how he doesn't like the segment we do."

"Oh, that sucks," she says, sounding disappointed.

"That was the gist of it. But here's the thing. A few months ago, it would have gotten in my head. One little email would have made me doubt my commitment to the show. Today? I don't give a shit." I lean back in my chair and grin, feeling like all is right in the world.

"You don't?"

I shake my head. "Don't care. Not bothered. You know why?"

"Why?" Her tone is curious.

"He's just one viewer. I can't please everyone. I do a damn fine job at work, and that hasn't changed since I started seeing you."

"Oh. That's good that you feel that way," she says, sounding nervous, maybe surprised.

I get it. She's not expecting this from me. I've made my concerns clear from the start. And I need to make it clear I don't have them anymore. "What I'm trying to say is I'm over the trust issues. I'm not going to let them get in my way anymore."

"You're not?"

I laugh. "Why do you sound so surprised?"

"Sorry. I . . . just wasn't expecting this right now. My mind is still in work mode."

"No worries. We can talk tonight. It's karaoke night. I'm going out with Cooper and some other friends. Would love to have you join us."

"Sure. Just text me the details."

My work line lights up. When I see the area code, I sit up straighter. "Shoot. That's Zander Kendrick's manager."

"Go, go. I know you've been waiting for this call."

I say goodbye and pick up the work line.

His manager is the chattiest fellow. He's also in

town and wants to have lunch to discuss the segment. Today.

We pick a place, and I tell him I'm on my way.

As I head out of the office, I send McKenna a text.

Chris: Heading to see Zander's manager now about the segment. Gomez Hawks at eight p.m. See you there.

She doesn't answer right away, and when I reach the restaurant, she's only sent one word.

McKenna: Sure.

No exclamation point. No smiley face.

Huh.

I note the oddity, but I don't focus on it. Instead, I head inside and focus on the meeting I'd been hoping to snag for a month now.

Besides, women are hard to read, even once you've fallen in love with one.

29

MCKENNA

It's no big deal.

I'm not rattled by that call.

Not one bit.

I don't mean the viewer's email. Chris is right on that score. You can't let those things get to you. That comment didn't bother him, and it doesn't bother me.

I mean the BIG ISSUE.

The "I'm over my trust issues" issue.

My heart hammers, my pulse spikes, and holy shit, I'm sweating.

I don't sweat. I'm not a nervous sweat-type person. But when I tug at my pastel-yellow blouse, it feels like it's sticking to me.

I head to my bedroom, appraising it in the mirror as Ms. Pac-Man trudges behind. "Ugh. Yellow is my worst color. Why did I pick yellow today?"

She slumps down on her dog bed without comment. At least she doesn't say *I told you so*. Surely she's advised me against yellow.

Did I listen? Evidently not.

I unbutton it furiously, missing a button and cursing. "Stupid buttons," I mutter.

Fumbling the traitorous button through the hole, I toss the shirt in the laundry and fan my face with my hand. Why is it so hot?

I head to the bathroom, grab a washcloth, and blot it over my chest and under my armpits.

"Breathe," I tell my red-faced reflection.

Ms. Pac-Man's nails scratch the floor as she follows me, tilting her head quizzically.

"What the hell is wrong with me?"

She quirks her snout the other direction.

"I don't know," I answer, my voice wobbly.

I don't know what's wrong with me.

I shuffle to my closet, snag a peach Free People top, tug it on, and force myself to take a deep breath.

Or rather, to gulp in air like a fish out of water.

That's how I feel.

Like I have gills on land.

Like I'm flopping around on shore without legs.

I crouch to Ms. Pac-Man, my center of gravity, and give her a hug, searching for a fixed point when my world is spinning weirdly off-kilter. "I just need to do something familiar. Something I'm used to, right?"

She rubs her cheek against my chest.

"I'll go to The Best Diner in the City. I'll take a lunch break. All by myself. Good idea, right?" I grab my lucky bag, kiss her goodbye, and hightail it out of my house, driving to the diner.

I hunt for my usual spot, but the block is packed.

The next one is too.

Where the hell is my parking good fortune?

I spot a free space and jerk my car into it, marching to the diner and cursing karma for screwing me over. For deserting me when what I need is to sit down, order some food, and remind myself that feelings aren't the devil.

Even though they are. They so are.

The hostess greets me by name, shows me to my regular table, and asks if I want a Diet Coke.

I relax my shoulders and visualize the knots of panic unknotting. I can do this. I can recalibrate to pre-wigging-out.

"Yes, please. And a house salad with French fries."

"Have that out in a jiff."

She takes off, and I spread the napkin in my lap. Yup. Fries and a salad. I'm all good. I'm not crazy. I'm completely not freaking out over *all the strings*.

I'm fine.

I can handle strings.

I just didn't think our relationship would have them so soon.

Now that he's admitted them, there are more leaks in the dam of my feelings than I have fingers to plug them with. But I have to try to dig my nails in and hold on.

"Oh, hey, McKenna."

I look up to see the girl-child, Amber, decked out in her pink sweat suit, smiling and waving.

The woman my ex-fiancé picked over me.

The living, breathing manifestation of all that I never was to the man I thought I'd marry.

My throat tightens, and the walls of the diner close in. They constrict the way I expected them to when I saw her here before.

I was supposed to be married to her husband. A little more than a year ago, I was ready to walk down the aisle to him. I thought I'd be done with dating forever. I thought Todd and I would be a family.

Now, he's *her* family, and I'm here, trying to figure out what to do with this colossal onslaught of monster-size feelings.

Oh shit.

These feelings for Chris are way bigger than the ones I had for Todd. Deeper than what I felt for him. Bigger, crazier, wilder. And so unexpected. So much more than fun. More than games. More than *no strings*.

These feelings have all the strings, and the last time I felt even close to this way, I was blindsided, bitch-slapped, and left with two KitchenAid mixers I didn't need.

I don't even know what to do with one.

"Hi, Amber." The greeting comes out stilted.

"You were so right about this place. It's wonderful. I've started coming here since that first time I saw you, and I love, love, love it."

"That's great, great, great," I say, then I want to slap myself. I don't mock people, even people who steal grooms.

But she's not the one I was mad at a little more than a year ago.

Todd was.

Only, I got over him.

I've 100 percent moved on from him.

But I haven't moved on from being human.

I can't move on from that. And because I'm human, I'm not immune to falling, after all. I've fallen hard and big and recklessly.

Now all I can think is—what if the same thing happens again? What if Chris finds someone funnier, smarter, more interesting? Someone who loves deeper, better, more?

What if I'm left behind again?

Fear reopens the wound inside me that had healed but not scarred over, and it's raw, like insecurity is rubbing salt in it.

Somehow I swallow past the hurt in my throat. "Glad you like it," I choke out, walking back my snitty reply so I don't have to add one more thing to feel awful about today.

Amber flashes a cordial smile and walks away.

I eat, and the salad tastes like cardboard, the Diet Coke seems flat, and the fries are anti-orgasmic.

When I leave, I go to the bakery and decide the only thing that could make me feel better is a cupcake. I order a chocolate buttercream and stuff it in my mouth.

But it doesn't remove the self-doubt that's formed an ulcer in my heart.

30

CHRIS

The interview is locked in for later this week.

The surf report for this afternoon appears top-notch.

And karaoke night is always a good time. Plus, I get to introduce my girl to my friends.

There's only one little hiccup.

The girl has gone radio silent.

I text her after lunch with the good news regarding Zander.

No reply.

I text her that afternoon telling her the ratings are strong for the segments.

Nada.

I tap out a third text then decide I'm a wuss. Something is wrong, and I need to man up and call her.

It rings five times.

She answers with a muffled *hey*.

"Hey," I say sympathetically, because she must be sick. "Are you okay? Do you have a cold or something?"

"No."

"What's wrong, babe?"

"Nothing. Just napping."

I arch a brow. Don't get me wrong—naps are awesome. But I have a hard time reconciling the bright and effervescent McKenna with someone who sleeps during the daytime. "I didn't know you were into afternoon naps."

"I'm not."

My Spidey-sense goes on full alert, and I sit up straight in my desk chair. "What's wrong?"

She heaves a sigh. "I don't think I can go to karaoke tonight."

"Okay, that's fine. But is something else wrong?"

"I just . . . Everything is happening so fast. I think I need a night to . . . figure it out."

I freeze.

Brace like I'm about to get pounded by a killer wave.

She's breaking up with me.

I swallow hard and try to form words. "What do you need to figure out?"

"This. Us. Everything. Why fries taste bad, and Diet Coke is flat, and cupcakes made me sick."

Ah, maybe she is ill. "So you are sick? Do you need something? Some soup? I can bring you food or crackers or anything you need."

She whimpers. "You're too perfect. This is too good to be true. I like you too much. I have to go."

She hangs up.

I stare at the phone like it's relaying radio signals in Martian.

Because that made zero sense.

I hit redial, but it goes straight to voicemail.

Now that? That makes sense. That translates to only one thing—she doesn't want to hear from me.

31

MCKENNA

So this is what having a meltdown is like. It's about blankets and dog cuddles and sad music blasting out all the noise in my head. It's Elvis and Billie Holliday bathing my brain in sad songs, tunes of love that'll never be. Love gone awry. Love that's broken.

Because a little hurt is better than a big hurt.

And I've had the big hurt.

I simply can't endure a bigger one, or even the risk of it. And with Chris, the hurt would be a doozy. It's best to wrap myself in layers of Kevlar now by going through life alone. Solo is way safer.

After about three hours of burrowing under my covers and feeding the kernel of sadness inside me, I spring out of bed, lit up with an idea.

Meltdowns need fashion.

I forage through the new shipment of clothes sent by brands wanting features on my site. For my solo fashion show, I blast a new and old girl-power mélange of Cyndi Lauper and P!nk and Billie Holiday, singing along with the ladies as I try on jeans and skirts and sweaters. With just the right outfit, I am armor-clad. Fashion is a shield. Lift up your chin, hold your head high, and drape yourself in discount designer wear. That's how you make it through your new life as a solo act. Or, really, my pre-Chris life. That's what I'll be— alone and fabulous, never hurt, always happy.

I toss a blue silk scarf around my neck and just as I spin around to ask Ms. Pac-Man's opinion, she launches herself off the bed, skids across the hardwood floor, and fishtails like a bus into the living room. Curiosity gets the better of me, so I follow her. She's scrabbling at the windowsill, barking her snout off.

"What is it, girl? A squirrel? Or is it the horny pug?" I make my way to her side, and my eyes pop when I see what's causing the commotion.

A devil cat, perched on the railing.

But a devil cat who belongs to my friend.

I race to the front door, yank it open, and dart across the stoop. But Chaucer is wily for a reason. He's possessed.

He swats a plant off Hayden's front stoop, knocking the tiny terra-cotta fern to its death, then he leaps off the porch.

"Oh no, you don't."

I'm not fast. I'm not agile. But I've had enough of that cat's troublemaking.

He scrambles under the stoop, and I cackle. There's only one way out, and I'm blocking it. "Ha. You're cornered, buddy."

Crawling under the stoop in my new jeans and silky

scarf, I lunge for him, thrusting out an arm and grabbing.

He slinks back, but he's cornered. I grab his scruff, tug him out, and then cradle him.

"It's okay. Let's get you inside," I tell him, switching gears immediately to a soft, cooing tone.

He remains stiff in my arms, but lets me carry him. I rap on Hayden's door with my elbow, and seconds later, Lena yanks it open.

"Chaucer!" She holds out her arms and reaches for him. He slides into her grasp, kicking up the purr-o-meter and rubbing his face against her, as if he's not the most dastardly animal of all time. I swear, this cat has nine lives and nine personalities.

"Thank you, McKenna." Lena bats her eyes at me. "I was worried. I couldn't find him when I got home from my Spanish lesson, but . . ." She glances around. "I think I might have accidentally let him out. I was just about to go looking for him."

"Well, here he is," I say, releasing a deep breath.

She kisses the top of his head. "Want to come in?"

I pretty much already am, so I close the door behind me. "Is your mom around?"

Lena shakes her head as she coddles the cat, petting his chin. "She'll be home in a few minutes. Dad is working late. Do you want some rice and sautéed garbanzo beans? I was going to make some for a snack."

"That's what you eat for a snack?"

"It's tasty." She narrows her eyes. "What happened to you? You don't look good."

I sigh. "It's a long story."

"Does it involve the guy you really like?"

I blink. How is this child so observant? "Why do you say that?"

"The way you sigh and seem all out of sorts. It makes me wonder if it's about a boy."

"It's nothing."

"Hmm. I'm not sure I believe that."

I shake my head, amused. "You're your mother's daughter, you know that, right?"

She smiles, heads to the couch, pats it, and tells me to sit. Chaucer curls up in her lap. "What's the deal?"

"I really like him," I blurt out, then I correct. "Wait, I think I love him."

"That's good, then."

"Why is that good? Love is awful and terrible, and it eats you alive."

"You're just saying that because of your ex, who's a big turd," she says.

I stare at her. "Excuse me?"

She lowers her voice. "Well, you don't want me to say what you and my mom really call him."

I shake my head vehemently. "You're right, I don't."

"You can't let him get you down though. It'd be like if I let myself believe all cats are as crazy as this one."

"But this cat *is* crazy."

"Yet I love him, and he loves me, and that's all that matters."

And I might officially be more confused. A door clicks open, and I snap my gaze toward it. Hayden walks in, eyes me, Lena, and my clothes. "Let me guess.

You're wallowing in self-pity and the utter terror of admitting you're in love again."

"My God, are you a witch? Can you read minds?"

She shakes her head. "No. I heard the last few things you two said as I opened the door."

Hayden moves around the couch, sinks down between us, kisses her daughter's forehead, then turns to me. "Tell me how you're your own worst enemy."

"She thinks not being in love with the guy she likes is better than being in love with him," Lena says, confidently summing up our brief conversation.

Hayden arches a brow, studying me. "Is that so?"

I shrug an admission. "I'll just get hurt again. Why bother?"

"Oh, sweetie. Tell me what happened."

Hayden asks Lena to leave, and when she's in her room, I spill all, detailing the phone call and Chris's words and seeing Amber and the terrible taste of fries and the utter horror that the whole damn day has wrought on me.

She pulls me in for a hug, pets my hair, then speaks softly. "I love you, and I'm only saying this because I love you, but if you let him get away, you're going to regret it for the rest of your life."

I jerk my head up. "I am?"

She exhales heavily. "Don't let him get away. Love is scary and terrifying and wonderful and enchanting all at the same damn time."

Worry tugs at me, threatening to lure me down into the blanket cave again. Fear of heartbreak is so damn powerful and paralyzing. "But what if ..."

"What if he's your sailboat in the moonlight?"

Those words—they hook into me, playing notes and chords inside me, hitting all my hopes and dreams. The ones I keep locked up, but the ones that are so real.

She shakes her head, squeezes my hand. "Love is one giant what-if. You might get hurt again, but you might also love more, feel more, give more. You might find your capacity to love expands and deepens. There's never a guarantee you won't get hurt. There's never a guarantee about anything. But that's what makes it so worthwhile. You get up and give it your all because of that chance for joy and happiness and that feeling that only comes from falling in love with someone who loves you back as wildly, as wondrously, and as deeply as you love him."

My heart army-crawls up my throat, and tears rim my eyes. "Stop it," I choke out.

"Stop what?"

"Stop being so right all the time."

She pulls me in for another hug. "It comes with age. I'm like a good wine."

I stay in her embrace for a few minutes, savoring the comfort of friendship. Her friendship, and Erin's and Julia's too, as well as Andy's and even Lena's—and certainly Ms. Pac-Man's—got me through a dark, terrible heartbreak.

I'm on the other side. I've been on it for a while now.

I'm better.

I'm happier.

I can either fall back into the familiar and keep my

heart on lockdown, wrapped up, insulated, and safe from the world.

Or I can unlock it and let it free.

Andy was right when he said I have the key.

I do.

All I have to do now is turn it.

32

CHRIS

Cooper kicks ass crooning Foreigner. Even I have to admit that. I say as much to our friend Violet, who's cheering him on during the chorus of the rock anthem.

"The man can sing," I say.

"He sure can," she says, and when she watches him, I swear she has stars in her eyes. Someday those two are going to realize they have it bad for each other.

When he's done, I glance at my phone, hopeful that McKenna will have reached out.

But the screen is empty. No text messages, and no missed calls.

I sigh heavily and rake a hand through my hair as Cooper makes his way off the stage, joining the crew at the table. He takes a bow, hamming it up, then flops down in a chair. He chats with Violet for a minute, and I check my phone once more.

He jerks his head toward me. "Just call her. Or better yet, go see her."

I shoot him a look. "What are you talking about?"

"You're checking your phone every five minutes. Your woman isn't here. Something went wrong. Go find her, and sort it out."

"It's not that easy," I say.

He moves his chair, pulling it away from the table and staring at me with serious brown eyes. "Isn't it?"

I shrug. "It's . . . complicated. She's . . ." I don't want to say more. I feel like I'm violating her trust.

Cooper waves a hand like he's a magician and is vanishing all these problems. "She's worried. She's freaking out. She's afraid. Something like that. The point is—do what you two always talk about on your show. *Communicate.* Be direct. Figure out if she's going to move forward with you or not. And if you don't want to do that, I'm going to have to take away your phone so you can't look at it anymore."

I stuff it in my back pocket and hold up my hands. "Fine. I'm done."

"Good. Now get your ass out of here, find your woman, and sort out whatever went down."

I don't need to cogitate on his advice. I know he's right. Hell, if I walked into the lioness den at The Tiki Bar, I can go to McKenna's goddamn house and find out where she stands. Is she in or out? That's a simple question. You're either willing to be in love or you're not. I need to make sure she's crystal clear on where I stand and what I want. Telling her I'm over my trust issues wasn't enough. I need to tell her I'm in love with her, and I want our *thing* to be the real thing. The one and only thing.

I stand, ready to head to her place, when someone taps on the microphone and the familiar opening notes of an Elvis tune float through the joint.

33

MCKENNA

I shower first.

I can't waltz in and find my man in my cat-chasing clothes.

Plus, I need a new outfit. When I get out of the shower, dry off, and track down a fabulous pink lace bra-and-undie set, there's a knock on my door. I pull on the silky items, wrap the towel around me, and head to the door. Peering through the peephole, I find three wiseasses making goofy faces at me.

I yank open the door, letting Julia, Erin, and Hayden inside.

"To what do I owe the pleasure of this visit?"

Julia points her thumb at Hayden. "This girl called and told us what went down."

Erin nods crisply. "We're here to babysit."

"I need a babysitter now?"

"Oh, hell yeah," Erin says, spinning me around and gently shoving me by the shoulders back to my bedroom.

"We are not letting you burrow your way out of this," Julia declares.

"I'm doing it, I'm doing it."

"I'll believe that when I put your butt in a Lyft and take you to Gomez Hawk's myself," Erin says.

I huff, but I'm smiling, loving that they're here, looking out for me.

A few minutes later, I slide into an A-line champagne-colored minidress that's shorter than sin and makes a statement—I'm a woman who goes after what she wants.

I add a pair of black ankle boots and my rose-gold bracelet. Then I dry my hair, put on makeup, and grab a clutch. When I reach the front door, nerves grapple me and my momentum falters.

"Oh no, you don't," Julia says.

I breathe in, reminding myself it's worth it.

The chance is worth it.

I'm worth it.

Julia and Erin order a car, and we say goodbye to Hayden. They slide into the ride with me as we head across the city.

"You're like my probation officers."

Julia nods. "Yup. We are."

When we reach the karaoke bar in Japantown and head inside, Julia kisses one cheek, Erin kisses the other, and they wish me luck.

But it's not luck I need.

It's strength and courage.

To love again after heartbreak.

To try again after hurt.

I might have had a little meltdown—okay, a big, fat, hairy one—but I'm here, ready to try again.

In the entryway of the karaoke bar, I ask the hostess for a favor and tell her what I need. She smiles and says she'll gladly help.

As a guy finishes up a Foreigner tune, the hostess tells me there will be one more song, then it's my turn.

She guides me backstage and hands me a mic. I peek around the velvet curtain. My heart skips when I see Chris.

It frolics.

It runs.

It wants to throw itself at him.

Except he looks sad.

And empty.

And it hits me—I did that to him. I made him feel like that. Like I didn't want him the same way he wants me.

I need this song to end. I need to get out there and tell him in a song that I do want him in every way. I hate the sadness in his eyes, the slump in his shoulders. And I'm going to make it right. Because he's over his trust issues, and I'm choosing to be over my fear.

The song ends, and as soon as the opening notes of "Can't Help Falling In Love" begin, I stride onstage.

Awash in nerves and hope at the same damn time.

Like Hayden said, love is both of those all at once. And you have to be strong enough to choose it.

I take one final breath, then I meet Chris's gaze and bring the mic to my mouth. I do my best imitation of the King as he sings about fools rushing in. The lyrics swoop into me, and even though I don't sound like Elvis, the look on Chris's face as he watches me kindles a fire in my soul.

Yes, Elvis, some things are meant to be. Like falling in love against your wishes. Against your better judgment. Against all your plans to do the opposite.

This time I'm not going to hide. I'm going to rush in, fool or not.

And when I reach the chorus, I'm not alone.

Chris walks to the stage, his eyes on me, his pace confident, his intentions clear. He steps up, joins me at the mic, and we sing the rest of the song together.

When it ends, I hear someone shout, "Kiss the girl!"

I laugh, butterflies fluttering in every cell of my body as I lower the mic and turn to face Chris. "By the way, I'm in love with you."

Grinning, he slides a hand around my waist. "I kind of figured that out. And I'm in love with you."

He kisses me in front of the crowd, in front of his friends, and it feels like a declaration. Like he's saying I'm his, and he's mine, and that's how it's going to be.

That sounds about right to me.

He deepens the kiss, and before I know it, we are all lips and tongue and teeth crashing into each other in an anthemic song of kissing, a big, epic tune of joy and passion and hope. Of falling in love again. Of letting go and starting over.

I am flying high right now, ready to head into the great unknown. Ready and eager.

* * *

We don't stop at Elvis.

We attack a whole screenful of songs, belting the guy and girl parts in "Love Shack" like we're now a singing duo, then performing The Human League's "Don't You Want Me." Then the whole group of us—Chris, his friends, Erin, Julia, and I—head back onstage after another round of drinks, and we do our best full-on rocker salute as we air-guitar our way through one of the best karaoke tunes ever—Bon Jovi's "Livin' on a Prayer."

Matching the words in the song, Chris takes my hand. I feel the music fill me up, and I swear, just like the song promises, we'll make it.

After, we go to the bar, laughing and kissing. He brushes my hair off my cheek and threads his fingers in my locks. "What do you say we get out of here?"

"What did you have in mind?"

He loops his hands around my neck, bringing my face to this. "There's this girl I'm in love with. And I'd really like to be alone with her right now."

Tingles. Everywhere.

We go to my home, and our clothes fly off in a flurry. I pull him down on my bed, bring him close, and wrap my arms around his neck. "Make love to me," I whisper, the words pricking at me with the sheer vulnerability of them.

"Always," he says, and it feels like a promise we'll both keep.

Later, when we're spent and curled up together, Ms. Pac-Man jumps on the bed, licks Chris's face, and flops down next to him.

"What did you just say?" I ask her.

"*I like him. He's a keeper*," I reply in the dog's voice.

He rolls over, gives her a smooch on the snout, and says, "Back at you."

And I fall in love even deeper.

34

CHRIS

Epilogue
Several months later

I watch from the street corner. Two deliverymen wait outside on McKenna's steps as she arrives home from a business meeting.

One of those guys walks up to her, presumably asking her name.

She nods.

He tells her, I suspect, that he has a delivery for her, and she stops and waits.

I smile, ridiculously pleased with the delivery in question.

The guy returns to the truck and wheels a dolly down the ramp. When he's halfway, McKenna realizes what's on it.

"Oh my God!" She's so loud, I can hear her as she

claps her hand to her mouth and jumps in excitement.

I walk down the block, heading straight to her. "Built it myself."

She spins around, and I'm in front of her. "You did?"

I pat the side of the *Q*Bert* machine. "I had a feeling you might like your own."

Fifteen minutes later, the delivery guys are gone, and there's a gorgeous new game in her living room.

"It's one hundred percent authentic," I say, handing the woman I adore a bag of quarters. "But no freebies. You have to pay this beast every time."

Her wild bluish-hazel eyes light up as she reaches for a quarter. "I want to play now."

Her excitement thrills me, makes me even more sure that this is right—that this is how it should be.

I clasp a hand over hers. "There's one thing I should let you know though. I tested it out first. Just to make sure it worked. You'll have to beat my high score."

"You're so cruel."

"I am the absolute worst."

"Fine," she huffs, pretending to be annoyed. "What's the score I have to beat?"

As I tap the screen to show her, a flock of nerves lands briefly in my chest, but they fly away quickly.

I'm ready.

When she stares at the score, she gasps.

Turns around.

Drops her jaw. "Seriously?"

I'm so serious I'm down on one knee. The score is high, and the name of the winner is "MARRY ME."

I'm pretty damn proud of what we've built.

I'll be the happiest guy around if she says yes.

"I've been falling for you since the day I met you, McKenna." I reach into my pocket and take out a dark velvet box. I flip it open and show her the ring, a vintage-style cut that's perfect for her. "And I don't plan to ever stop falling in love with you. Will you be my wife?"

She falls to her knees, knocks me down so I'm sitting, and sinks into my lap, then throws her arms around me. I can feel her tears on my cheeks.

"Yes," she whispers. "I don't plan to stop either."

She pulls back, and I slide on the ring. She beams and can't stop looking at it. Then she quirks up a brow. "Hey, do I have to take your name? Because McKenna McCormick would be quite silly."

"Take my name or don't take my name. All I care is that you're mine forever. For always."

"I am. I'm yours. Always."

35

MCKENNA

Another Epilogue

A few months later

I should be terrified to walk down the aisle. But I'm not. I don't have a shred of doubt inside me. All I feel is the faith, hope, and certainty in this choice. Marrying the man I'm madly in love with is awesome.

"Don't you agree?" I ask Ms. Pac-Man, who sits patiently by my side as I apply my lip gloss then twirl once in front of the antique gilded mirror in my room here at the Golden Gate Club in the Presidio, near the water.

"You look so beautiful, and this dress is so completely you," Julia tells me. She's seen the dress many times—she helped me pick it out.

I'm in love with it too. Not that I have a hard time

falling in love with clothes, but this one was insta-love. With a smooth A-line and a lacy bodice, it's a decadent mix of sexy, stylish, and bridal.

We leave the suite, my faithful dog by my side. My three bridesmaids are with us as well—Hayden and Erin, and Chris's sister, Jill, who's now become a good friend of mine. We head through the expansive grounds of the hotel to the bluff overlooking the water. The ocean waves loll peacefully against the shore, and the afternoon sun warms us. White chairs are spread across the lawn, and all my friends and family are here.

I kind of want to run down the aisle because I'm so damn ready to be that man's wife. But I control myself and wait patiently at the edge of the chairs as my bridesmaids, and then my sister, the maid-of-honor, walk across the white runner rolled out on the lawn.

When the King croons, I take the first step toward my soon-to-be husband. A huge, ridiculous smile spreads across my face because Chris is incredibly handsome in his tux.

He waits for me at the edge of the bluff as the last words of the song fade. I reach his side, and his smile is as wide as mine.

"You're beautiful. I can't wait to be married to you," he whispers.

Yes, he was worth taking a flying leap for. He's worth getting over all my fears. He's worth everything to me.

The justice of the peace clears his throat and begins. "I'm told by the couple that we have a cat to thank for this union. But they decided not to bring

Chaucer along to the ceremony, and as your highly allergic officiant, I thank you many times over for that."

We both laugh, and so do the guests.

"When Hayden's cat swatted McKenna's hard drive many months ago, she thought she merely had a damaged electronic device. But that dastardly cat's attack was the best thing that ever happened to her because it's the reason she met Chris, the man who's about to become her husband."

"If Chaucer were here today, I'd high-five him," Chris says.

"But it's because of the two of them that they stayed together. Through doubt, through uncertainty, and through starting over. Now they're here, ready to be together always."

The justice of the peace segues into the vows. "Do you, Chris McCormick, promise to love, cherish, and honor McKenna Bell for the rest of your days?"

"Absolutely," he answers, and my heart swells with joy as I savor his words.

"And do you, McKenna, promise to love, cherish, and honor Chris for the rest of your days?"

"Every single day."

"Now it is time to exchange the rings."

I turn my attention to the crowd, and there's Ms. Pac-Man, waiting dutifully at the end of the chairs.

"Come here, girl," I call out, and my dog trots along the aisle.

When she reaches us, Chris removes the rings from the pouch on her collar. She's a good girl; she listens to him now too. He taught her how to surf, and there is nothing cuter than my sexy guy and my dog riding the Pacific waves.

Ms. Pac-Man lies at our feet as Chris slides the wedding band onto my finger, and I do the same for him.

The justice of the peace finishes the ceremony with these final words: "McKenna Bell and Chris McCormick, I now pronounce you husband and wife. You may kiss the bride."

Chris kisses me, and it's as amazing as our first time, as our second, as our third. It's a kiss that curls my toes, sweeps me off my feet, and melts me.

We dance and toast and eat French fries and other yummy delicacies, and then there's a karaoke contest. It's not a fair one, though, because Chris's sister just won a Tony for Best Actress in a Musical, but that's why we want to hear her sing. She belts out an amazing rendition of "Overjoyed" by Matchbox Twenty that gives me chills, her voice carrying throughout the tent and far across the ocean, I'm sure.

Late into the night, Chris pulls me aside, and we dance under the twinkling lights.

"Hey, wife." He loops his arms around my waist.

"Hi, husband," I say, curving a hand around his neck.

"Are you having a good time?"

I pretend to ponder his question. "Hmm. There are French fries with forty-seven varieties of dipping sauce, including orgasmic ketchup. All my friends are here, and so is my dog. And I'm with my favorite person in the whole world. I'm having the time of my life." I give him a cheeky smile. "I still want to beat you at *Q*bert* though."

"You have a lifetime to do that," he says then spins me around and brings me in close for another kiss.

I do have a lifetime with him. I have something more too—faith that we'll go the distance.

As the King would say, some things are meant to be.

I take his hand as we leave the dance floor later that night, stepping into our forever.

THE END

Curious about Cooper's romance? He has a story to tell in the USA Today Bestseller MOST VALUABLE PLAYBOY, available everywhere! Chris's sister Jill has a love story in PLAYING WITH HER HEART! Sign up for my newsletter to make sure you don't miss my next hot new book!

That's the second-chance romantic comedy Satisfaction Guaranteed, a sexy, hilarious rom-com told in the guy's POV! If you loved Big Rock, you'll go nuts for this book!

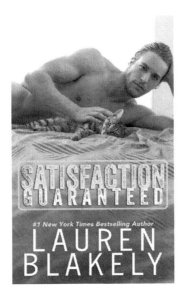

Prologue

Dude-bros will tell you the pinnacle of male sexual prowess is to make a woman meow.

I will tell you, that's a dumbass metaphor.

Literal, figurative, it's complete bullshit.

Cats meow when they're hurt, hungry, or just plain chatty. A feline might be stressed, pissed, or simply want you to open the goddamn bedroom door at night.

So, the cat's meow is a myth. I should know.

But the purr? The magical, mysterious, wondrous purr? The aural indication of pussycat pleasure? That's the mission impossible a man ought to be making come to life. Cats purr for a couple reasons, but the most common one is to show they're satisfied.

Yes, *satisfied*.

That's a man's job, and that's why I don't play small stakes kitty-cat games. No cat's meows, no pajamas either. My one goal when I get a woman between the sheets is to make her so immensely pleased that she purrs.

I'm not an over-and-out type of guy. There's no one-and-done for me. I'm a believer in delivering satisfaction in every way, in and out of the bedroom.

That's exactly what I want to do with a certain someone.

Trouble is, that someone is most definitely off-limits, so it's time to put a leash on this dog.

But then I learn something wildly unexpected about her, and there's no way I can turn away from that kind of challenge.

Chapter One

She's gorgeous. An absolute stunner, with captivating green eyes, high cheekbones, and strong legs. Her silky black hair is long and luxurious. She stretches, showing off her nubile body.

I can't keep my eyes off her.

Or my hands, for that matter.

I run a palm down her back, and she arches against me.

"Doesn't she seem rather . . . lethargic?" her mistress asks, concern etched in her eyes. I peer closely at the little lady in question.

Those whiskers. That tail. "Sabrina's mood seems fine. Her heart rate is perfect. Her fur looks great. I see one very healthy pussycat. Why do you think she's lethargic, Lydia?" I ask as the silky black feline swishes her tail back and forth, rubbing against my hand on the exam table.

Lydia fiddles with a necklace that dangles between her breasts. "She's not playing with her toys much."

"Does she normally like to play with toys?"

Lydia drags a hand down her chest. "Oh, she enjoys toys so very much."

Dammit. I walked right into that one.

But I'm practiced in the art of deadpan deflection. "Well, that would indicate she doesn't need my services. She seems full of energy here. Is there something else going on at home with her that I should be concerned about?"

Lydia doesn't look at the kitty. She flicks her chestnut hair off her shoulder, her eyes pinned on me, ignoring the vet tech in the room completely. "She seems to need a little more attention. I feel like that's what she's telling me."

I maintain my completely-unaware-of-her-double-meaning routine. "But *you* give her lots of attention?"

"I do, but it's solo, Doctor Goodman. I think she wants it from others, if you know what I mean."

Yep, I don't need to be Inspector Poirot to crack the mystery of that case. I figured it out the instant Lydia prowled into the exam room with a cat who is as fit as an Olympic athlete.

I slide around her efforts with a standard vet

answer: "Cats are fickle. Some want attention. Some are fine without it." Sabrina rubs her head against my hand, cranking up the volume as she marks me. But hey, she's allowed to. Also, cats like me. Dogs like me. I am an absolute animal magnet, and the feeling's quite mutual.

"See? She likes you. She might want affection from you . . ." Lydia's eyes take a long, lingering stroll up and down my body.

Time for the full-scale oblivion shield. There's a fine line between playing dumb and looking stupid, and as a veterinarian, I can't afford to look bad in front of clients. But as a man, I definitely need to pull off the clueless-to-her-advances act with a particular kind of balance and finesse.

I ask Jonathan, the tech, to hand me a thermometer.

"Of course, Doctor Goodman," he says, hamming it up as if it's his utter delight to deliver the device.

Meeting Lydia's gaze, I brandish the thermometer with a grin. "Sabrina might not be so keen on me after this."

This is the moment when Lydia will back down, I'm sure. They nearly all do when the mercury comes out.

Instead, Lydia emits a sort of *coo*, like a songbird. "Oh, I bet she'd love that. I'm up for . . . I mean, she's up for anything."

Jonathan snickers, and I sigh. I focus solely on the cat, rather than on this cat-and-mouse game of cat-and-woman sublimation. Fortunately, Sabrina's just fine, and I tell Lydia so when I'm through with the exam. I snap off my gloves, wash my hands, and tell her to keep an eye on her feline. "If anything changes, let us know."

She smiles seductively at me. "Oh, I will. My pussycat's health is quite important to me."

Stay stoic, Malone. You can do it. You've done it before. "Yes, I can see that."

She waggles her fingers. "And if anything changes for you, Doctor Goodman, let me know too."

Blank face. I give her the 100 percent tabula rasa. "Thanks for coming in today."

"I'm glad I did." She rakes her gaze over me. "You're a regular Doctor Doolittle."

I've only been called that, oh, twelve times a day. But it's a compliment of the highest order, so I treat it as such. "Thank you."

She takes a step closer, her stare dropping down, down, down. "Or should I call you Doctor Doolarge?"

I stifle a strangled chuckle—I don't want to give her any encouragement, especially since I do like her cat, as in the actual *feline*. "Let's stick to Doctor Goodman."

After I say goodbye to Lydia, Jonathan clears his throat, adopting a high-pitched feminine voice. "Tell me, Doctor Doolarge, is it *hard* being so good-looking?"

I laugh. "It's the family curse."

"And such a cross to bear. However do you manage?"

"It's not easy. Someday, I'll teach you."

"Yes, please. I want to know all your secrets." He shifts to all-business mode. "You have a few clients who requested phone calls."

I glance at the clock. It's almost closing time, and I have a show tonight. "No problem. I have time."

He hands me the call sheet, and I head to my office and pick up the phone. When I'm done, I swing by the front desk where Jonathan and our office manager, Sam, are debating the best spots for craft beer in the West Village.

"Hey, Doctor Doolarge," Jonathan says, leaning back in his chair, stroking a hand over his bearded jaw. "Got a hot date tonight?"

With her pink hair tied in a huge bun on top of her head, Sam shoots him a skeptical stare. "Don't ask him that. It's personal. You shouldn't pry." She turns to me, adopts a cheeky smile, then whispers, "But tell me. Are you meeting a secret lady at Gin Joint tonight?"

Laughing, I roll my eyes. "Just my sister and the mic."

"But it would make such a yummy story. Vet moonlights as lounge singer and meets the love of his life at underground speakeasy. I can see it now." She spreads her arms wide, making a marquee sign. "They'd want me to play her in the Broadway version of your life story."

Jonathan scoffs. "You can't even sing."

She shoots him a withering glare. "Please don't ruin my daydreams."

I rap my knuckles on the counter. "Speaking of dreams, I have a set tonight then a hot date with some paperwork. In fact, it's the sexiest, steamiest paperwork I've ever seen."

"Just a couple more days, right?" Sam crosses her fingers.

"Here's hoping," I add.

"Me too," Jonathan says.

I head for the door, grabbing the handle.

Jonathan calls out, "Have fun with your paperwork, Dr. Doolarge." Every syllable drips with mockery.

I will never live down this new nickname with my staff.

But if the deal goes through, I can live with it.

What's a nickname when you're about to make your dreams come true?

TOO GOOD TO BE TRUE

Dear Reader,

Please enjoy TOO GOOD TO BE TRUE, a short novella from the ONE LOVE series.

xoxo
   Lauren

TOO GOOD TO BE TRUE

BY LAUREN BLAKELY

A standalone novella in the One Love series

She's wary of love. He's been burned. But when a matchmaker connects these two jaded New Yorkers, sparks fly and chemistry crackles from the first date. Can this kind of insta-connection be the real thing? Or is it too good to be true? Find out in this delicious novella from #1 NYT bestselling author Lauren Blakely!

1

OLIVIA

Do I want to try it?

My brother asked me that very question when he invited me to check out a prototype for his new home automation system.

This is no Alexa. This is no Google Home. His home automation system supposedly answers your most annoying emails, makes you an omelet, and even folds your laundry.

Well, in my dream life it does.

Geek that I am, naturally I said "hell to the yes" when he invited me to take a test run. So here I am, race-walking across the blond hardwood floor of the lobby of his swank Gramercy Park building and pushing the button to his penthouse apartment.

When I reach the top floor, I practically vault down the hall to his place.

Can you say eager?

I bang on his door. He takes more than ten seconds

to answer, so I decide to act thoroughly annoyed when he finally does.

"Come on, come on, come on." I'm bouncing on my toes, making grabby hands.

He rolls his eyes from behind his black glasses. "Overeager much?"

He holds the door open for me. I sweep in, my eyes like lasers scanning for the little white device. "You can't dangle something as cool as the ultimate home automation in front of me and expect me not to jump all over it and want to play with it. I only strapped a jetpack on and flew down to touch it."

He laughs, escorting me to the living room. He knows that, just like him, I love all sorts of electronics, gadgets, gizmos, and toys, and have ever since we were kids, fighting over all sorts of various game consoles. Since I'm the oldest, with two twin brothers, I usually beat them.

And I beat them up.

Someone had to put the little evil geniuses in their place. Lately, it's hard to put Dylan in his place since he's been traveling for business. But when he returns, I fully intend to kick his butt in our softball league.

"True, true," Flynn says thoughtfully. "What was I thinking? You and Dylan are both geeks like me."

I hold up a fist for knocking. "Dude, we are so nerdy. Also, FYI: nerds rule."

He scoffs authoritatively. "You know it. Nerd or bust."

I spy the device on the coffee table. My eyes widen

and I hold out my hands, like I'm caught in a tractor beam. "Take me to your leader."

"Kate is all yours," he says, using the name of the automation device.

I park myself in the leather couch and fire off questions.

"Kate, tell me a dog joke."

"Kate, make me a sandwich."

"Kate, what's the weather like in Bora Bora?"

She answers each one with panache.

What's more amazing than a talking dog? A spelling bee.

Okay, you're a sandwich.

And . . .

Perfect, you should go there.

I glance at Flynn, who's rightfully proud of his new tech. "Kate knows the answers to everything. I'm booking a flight now."

Flynn nods his agreement. "Bora Bora is always a good idea. If anyone thinks otherwise, you should excise him or her from your life."

I tap my temple. "The Bora Bora litmus test. I'm filing that away." I return my focus to the white disc. "Kate, make me a playlist of top pop songs."

As she preps some Ariana Grande and Katy Perry, Flynn groans and drops his head into his hand.

"No, please, no pop songs."

"I like pop."

"You need to try indie rock, I've told you."

I roll my eyes and launch into my best rendition of his favorite tunes. "Oh, my life is so sad, I flew with an eagle, and now I have a noose around my toes."

He cracks up and gives me the strangest look. "What on earth is that, Olivia?"

I answer like it's obvious. "That's what indie sounds like. A sad lament."

"Oh, well then, let me tell you what pop sounds like." Flynn adopts an intensely happy look, snapping his fingers, then sings a send-up of my music. "Oh, I want you. Yes I do. Yes, yes, yes, I do. Do do do do do do do do."

I laugh. "See, that's so fun to listen to! You should totally write that song."

"So we agree to disagree on music."

"But not the Bora Bora litmus test."

"Never the Bora Bora litmus test."

I spend the next hour playing with the device, and pronounce it is the coolest one I've ever seen. "But we have one more test for Kate."

"What is it?"

I hold my arms out wide, like I'm ready to make a pronouncement. "This will be the toughest test of all. Can she handle what I'm going to throw at her?"

Flynn gestures grandly. "Go for it."

I clear my throat, adopting a most serious tone. "Kate, find me a hot, smart, and kind guy. Must love animals. Be willing to try quirky new dates in New York City. Ideally, likes odd and interesting art installations. And be able to sustain a conversation about something other than himself."

Flynn's eyes bulge. "She's not a miracle worker," he says protectively. He's protective of the device.

Kate speaks back in her calming robotic voice, but

I've rattled her. "I'm sorry, that does not compute. Can you please try again?"

I crack up.

"You can't really expect her to do the impossible," Flynn says.

"I know, tell me about it."

He leans forward, hands on his knees. "So is dating getting you down?"

I sigh. "A little bit. It's kind of awful out there. Have you tried it lately?"

He shudders. "No, I'm practically on a sabbatical since Annie."

I shudder too, remembering Flynn's ex. She turned out to be completely using him, trying to sink her claws into his fortune. Not for nothing, but it's really hard for a tech multimillionaire to find somebody who likes him for him. My brother is rich as sin, and normally I don't feel bad for him, but on this count—never knowing if someone loves you for you or your money—my heart is heavy.

It's a poor little rich boy dilemma, as he calls it. Yet it's wholly real.

"But what about you? What's the latest from the minefield of dating?"

"Last night I went out with a handsome surgeon, who was all around pretty funny and smart. But it turns out he's into jazz music," I say, crinkling my nose. "He spent half the time telling me he loves to go to jazz clubs *and* to listen to jazz at home. I had to be honest— jazz is never going to be part of my life, so we're clearly not compatible. We'd never see each other."

Flynn gives me a look, takes a deep breath. "Olivia. But are you doing it again?"

"Doing what?" I ask, indignant. "Being direct and honest on dates about what works and doesn't work?"

"Are you sabotaging every date you go on?"

I sit up straight. "I do not do that."

He points at me. "Yes, you do."

"I don't care for jazz."

"I'm sure you could have found a work-around for his love of jazz. Instead, you sabotage. You've done that ever since Ron."

I huff. "Do you blame me? Ron was the ultimate douchenozzle. And he hid it well."

"'Douchenozzle' is a bit tame for that specimen. More like 'king of all the assholes ever.' It's not often you find a man who's not only a cheater but a serial cheater. He had affairs like it was an advent calendar."

A twinge of embarrassment stings my chest. "And that makes me the stupidest woman ever for missing the signs?"

Flynn moves next to me, squeezing my shoulder. "No. You liked the guy, and he was the Artful Dodger. It was hard to spot his deception at first. But ever since then, when you've met a guy here or there who seems somewhat decent, you always find something wrong with him. A smart and funny surgeon? But he likes jazz, so that's a dealbreaker? And then you tell him?"

"But I don't like jazz one bit," I say in a small voice.

"Look, I don't like jazz either. But I don't think it needs to be a line in the sand." He arches a brow. "Be honest with me. Are you constantly looking for what's wrong with a man so you won't get hurt again?"

I sigh, wishing it wasn't so obvious, but then Flynn knows me as well as anyone. "I was totally hoodwinked by Ron. I didn't see it coming, and I should have. What if it happens again?" I ask, my deepest worry coloring my tone.

"Anything can happen, but now you try to find something wrong with someone before you even start. You're never going to open yourself to what you want if you do that."

I cross my arms, exhale heavily. "Fine, maybe I do that, but look, I haven't met anybody that ticks all the boxes on my checklist. Or even three quarters. Hell, I'd settle for half. I don't even know if my dream guy exists."

He stares out the window, like he's considering a math problem. Since my brother solves math problems in his sleep, he snaps his fingers. "My buddy Patrick. His sister is a matchmaker."

"A real matchmaker? Like Yente?" I sing a few lines from *Fiddler on the Roof*.

"Of course, you have to sing that every time you see her. It's literally required. Why don't you try Evie? Let her know what you're looking for. Maybe she can find someone for you."

I've tried online dating. I've been set up by friends. I've been open to meeting men at the gym, at bookstores, even at the farmers market. But I've had no luck finding a jazz hater, animal lover, quirky-art fan, who's hot as hell and likes me.

"Admittedly, I'm kind of picky. Do you think I'm better off being single?"

"Olivia, you want to be happy. You want to find someone. Just call Evie. Her job is to find matches for picky people."

That sounds exactly like me.

And because I'm not boneheaded, I do call her. I meet with her the next day at a coffee shop.

She's everything you want in a matchmaker. She has a keen eye for people; she's perky, wildly outgoing, fantastically upbeat; and she knows everyone.

"Are my requirements just too crazy?" I ask after I've told her what I'm looking for.

Evie gives me a reassuring look and pats my hand. "No. You don't have requirements that are too hard to meet. What's too hard is to find a man like that online. But that's why you came to me." Her smile is radiant and full of confidence. "I have a few men in mind. Just give me a couple of days, and I promise I will do everything I can to find you the man of your dreams."

It sounds impossible to me.

2

HERB

"Hey there, little Cletus. You're doing great, and you look swell," I tell the teacup chihuahua with the burnished brown coat. He whimpers as I stroke a hand down his soft back. Cletus is resting in a cage after the five-month-old had a very important surgery today. "Don't worry," I whisper. "You won't miss them."

My vet tech snickers behind me. "Bet he will."

I roll my eyes at David as I turn around. "I see you're suffering from neutering sympathy. Shall I get him a pair of neuticles to make you feel better?"

"That would help me a lot, come to think of it."

"You do know he doesn't miss them?"

David grabs his crotch. "I'd miss mine."

"Then it's a good thing I'm not neutering you, isn't it?"

At twenty-three, David is still young, and his age might be why he still feels that associative pain that men often experience when a dog is neutered. At age thirty-four, and after thousands of spays and neuters,

I'm well beyond that. I don't get emotional over removing that particular part of a dog's anatomy. And I don't get weirded out.

It's all in a day's work.

David gives me a salute. "Yes, boss. Also, Cletus's foster mom is here."

"Great. I'll go chat with Evie." She's a regular foster for one of the city's nearby rescues, bringing in little dogs for their nip and tucks as they're getting ready to be adopted.

Gently, I scoop up the pup and carry the cone-headed boy to the lobby of my practice on the Upper East Side.

Evie waves brightly at me. "And how is the sweet little boy?"

"He did great."

Evie laughs. "Now, I always thought it was kind of funny to say that an animal did great during a surgery. Because, really, isn't it *you* who did great during a surgery?" She taps my shoulder affectionately.

She has a point.

And I concede to it, blowing on my fingernails for effect. "When you've got it, you've got it. No one snips dog balls better than this guy."

"Put that on your business card, Herb."

"It'll be my new tagline." I shift gears. "All right, you know the drill. Give him plenty of rest, make sure he takes it easy. He might not want to eat right away. And whatever you do, keep that lampshade on him."

Evie drops her face into the dog's tiny cone and

gives him a kiss. "I won't let you get out of your cone, I promise, Coney Boy."

"Give me a call if anything comes up, okay? Day or night. Doesn't matter."

"That sounds perfect." But before she turns to leave, she gives me a look. It's a look that says she has something on her mind. "Dr. Smith, I've been meaning to ask you something."

"I can see the wheels turning in your head."

She smiles, acknowledging that I'm right. "Have you started dating again? It's been more than a year or so since Sandy left."

"Yes, I've dated," I say, a little defensively. "I just haven't met the right person."

"It's hard to meet the right person. I hear you on that front." Her tone is sympathetic.

"I thought I *had* met the right person."

The thing is Sandy was a fantastic woman, and I can't fault her for leaving. She was offered a fantastic job in Beijing. She accepted and boarded a flight two weeks later without any fanfare or discussions about us continuing.

We'd been together for a year. We'd started making plans. And then her plan was to move halfway around the world, so that's what she did, ending us in one clean slice.

"But you can't let it get you down," Evie adds. "You are a prize."

I straighten my shoulders and flash an over-the-top smile. "Thank you. I always thought I'd look really nice paraded around onstage, perhaps given away at the end of a blue ribbon ceremony."

"We'll enter you in a dating contest." She sighs thoughtfully, her eyes narrowing a bit as she taps her chin with her free hand. "But I have other ideas for you."

"Fess up. Are you trying to enlist me into your stable again?"

She swats my arm affectionately. "Of course. I've only been trying to get you in my stable for ages. You know that. Smart, single, sweet as anything, clever, hot vet who does free spay and neuter clinics for the city's rescues? You are going to be in demand."

Since she's a premiere matchmaker, Evie's broached the subject before. I've been reluctant though. Maybe I've been nursing my wounds since my ex took off with barely a goodbye kiss. Or maybe a part of me figures if I can put myself through vet school, open a successful practice, and make it in Manhattan, I ought to be able to find a woman without a little assistance. "Honestly, I figured I'd meet someone the old-fashioned way, like how I met Sandy. We bumped into each other at a coffee shop. She nearly spilled her hot chocolate on me."

"Ah, the old rom-com meet-cute."

"Well, yeah. I suppose it was. So I assumed I'd meet someone new in a similar fashion."

"And how's that working out for you?"

I scratch my jaw, considering her question. "Badly."

"You don't say?"

"Do I detect a note of mockery?"

"No. I simply agree that it's as hard as differential calculus to hope to meet someone in person in a random, swoony, just-like-the-movies way."

"I've been on dates. Mostly setups from friends."

"And?"

I wince, shaking my head. "Dreadful. I'd rather bathe in molasses than go out with another *oh, Tonya knows so-and-so and so-and-so knows so-and-so*. And what it truly amounts to is this—your one single friend was pressured by his girlfriend or fiancée to set up her one single friend, and it doesn't matter if you have anything in common."

She nods sympathetically as she strokes Cletus's head. "That is indeed the problem with friends setting up friends simply by virtue of their relationship status. I, however, have a long list of lovely single ladies, and I only connect people I think—no, I'm sure—will go together like gin and tonic."

"I do like a good gin and tonic."

She smiles impishly. "I know. All my clients are vetted and interested in the real deal. And I know you're interested in that too."

"How do you know?" I'm curious why she says that, but truth be told, she nailed it on the head.

"That's what you wanted with Sandy. You're not somebody who goes out and plays the field, Herb."

She's right on that count. "That's true."

She stares at me, determination etched in her blue eyes. "So, what's it going to be, Mister Meow?"

I groan. "No. That nickname is unacceptable."

"I promise I won't call you that again if you'll let me match you."

"So it's coercion now, eh?" The woman is relentless with her cheer and optimism.

"Call it coercion, or call it kismet. Whatever you call it, I have the perfect woman for you."

I raise a skeptical brow. "What if she's boring?"

She shakes her head. "Not a chance."

I toss out another concern. "What if she's shallow?"

"She's bright and thoughtful."

And one more hurdle. "What if she, I dunno, smells?"

Evie leans in closer and taps my nose with her finger. "She smells pretty, you silly man."

Then the dealbreaker. "What if she doesn't like dogs?"

"Give me some credit. As if I'd set you up with someone who doesn't like dogs. The woman I have in mind is lovely. She's been looking to adopt just the right three-legged dog."

And my heart melts a little bit. Wait, wait. I can't. I can't fall for her that quickly, I don't even know her. "I suppose one date can't hurt. But I don't want to do dinner."

"Dinner is off the table."

"I don't want to do a wine tasting."

"Just say no to the vino."

"I don't want to do a beer tasting, and I don't want to do something that's like super hipster-y, like a mayonnaise tasting or pickle tasting."

"Got it. You probably don't want to do a carrot tasting either, then. Do you?"

"Do people really have carrot tastings?"

"Have you been to Brooklyn? They have everything these days."

"True that."

"You want to do something totally unconventional. Something that will let you know if you have chemistry."

That's the thing. I've done the whole typical three dates thing a handful of times ever since Sandy left, and I don't want to get on that merry-go-round again. "I just want to get on the merry-go-round once for one date, and I'll know after one date."

"Then it needs to be one spectacular date. Do you still like bizarre, oddball, quirky modern art?"

"Damn, you have a good memory."

"I have a memory for matches. Would you like to meet a smart, sarcastic, tech-savvy art lover who likes to discover all the interesting things about New York and who loves puzzles?"

My ears perk up. "I love puzzles."

3

OLIVIA

"How do I look?" I ask my brother, since he stopped by to pick up a book. Perfect opportunity to nab his opinion.

His green eyes light up with laughter and, admittedly, a whole ton of mockery. "How do you look?" he echoes as he tucks *Why We Sleep* under his arm.

I bristle. "I need a guy's opinion."

"And you asked me?" He points to his chest.

"I'm pretty sure you're a guy. Is there something you want to tell me? Did you swap your parts?"

"No, but my point is, I'm your brother. It basically disqualifies me from ever commenting on your appearance."

I huff. "Can you just tell me if I look good?"

"No, I actually can't tell you. I couldn't function any longer as a man in any way if I tell my sister she looks good. Fine, empirically, yes. You look good. But you also look stupid because you're my sister, and I have to think that."

"You legitimately cannot think your sister looks nice in something? I'm thirty, you're twenty-seven. We're not children anymore."

"Doesn't matter. Certain things can never change. You look fine. Sisters always look fine. I can't give you any other opinion than that."

I stare daggers at him. "Flynn, it's a good thing I like you. And you know what? I like myself too, so I am going to assume that I chose wisely in the fashion department."

He flashes a smile as he claps my shoulder. "There you go. That's the confident sis I know and love. You did choose wisely. Now go out and have a great time. I'm so psyched that you used Evie. I have a good feeling about this. Don't sabotage it."

"Who, me?" I ask ever so innocently. "I would never do that."

His expression goes stern. "I mean it, Liv."

I hold up my free hand in oath. "I promise. I installed an anti-sabotage shield on myself tonight. And I am going into this with eyes wide open."

"Be good," he says as he heads for the door. I say goodbye, then give myself a final once-over in the mirror.

Jeans look good, boots look sexy, cute top that slips off one shoulder is pretty, with a hint of something more. My brown hair sports a little wave as it curls over my shoulders.

"You are a thumbs-up," I tell my reflection.

I head downtown to Tribeca to meet Herb, the hot vet.

* * *

I arrive right on time, expecting him to be late. Most
people usually are. But when I see a tall, trim, toned,
handsome, as in the most handsome in the entire
universe, man standing in front of a light installation at
the Helen Williams Gallery, my breath catches.

There's no way that's him.

That guy in the dark jeans and a blue button-down
shirt that hugs his muscles has to be somebody else. I
bet he was flown in, shipped in from some foreign
country that grows good-looking men in meadows. He
was paid to stand around and simply radiate handsome. He has to be a model. There's no way that's actually Herb, the hot vet, standing under a fuchsia-pink
light, exactly where Evie said to look for him.

Herb is probably in the restroom and this stepped-
out-of-a-magazine-ad man is holding his spot.

But then Mr. Too Handsome for Words catches my
gaze. His lips quirk up in a lopsided smile that puts all
the other lopsided smiles in the entire universe to
shame. Because that is the crooked smile that defines
why crooked smiles are absolutely delicious. Already
my stomach is flipping, and I haven't even talked
to him.

"What do you think? Is pink my color?" he asks
from a few feet away, glancing up at the light.

God, I hope it's him. I walk closer. "I see you as
more of a magenta."

He gives me a thoughtful look. "That's too bad. I
was actually hoping perhaps I would be a periwinkle."

I laugh. "Do you know what periwinkle looks like?"

"No, isn't it a shade of, let me guess, blue?" He extends a hand. "I'm Herb Smith."

Praise the Lord. "I'm Olivia Parker."

Herb Smith is the most handsome man I've ever met, with his dark hair, square jaw, and blue eyes the sapphire color of perfect Bora Bora ocean. The man is to die for, and I don't believe in playing games. If I'm going to be up-front with the duds, I'll be direct with the un-duds.

"I didn't think the man standing under the light was actually going to be you," I admit, going for full truth.

"Why's that?"

I gulp, and then I bite off a big chunk of honesty, since what's the point in anything else? "You look like you were imported from the land of hot men."

He blinks. His eyes widen and sparkle, and then he says, "Wow. I didn't know that country existed."

"It's right between Goodlookingvia and Stunning-landenero. Just north of Beautifulcountria."

"I'd like to see your map of the world."

"I have it at home. But was that too forward? Calling you good-looking and objectifying you from the start? Want me to rewind and go again?"

"Hold on a second. You just complimented me for being too handsome, and you think that was too forward?"

"In case you think I'm only evaluating you based on your appearance," I say, since I had the impression from Evie that her services are more of the soul mate variety and less of the hop-on-the-hottie style.

He runs a hand lightly down my arm. "Judge me some more. I should be so lucky."

He drops his arm and I smile, the kind that stretches across my whole face. "In fact," he adds, "I hope you have a long list of traits you're going to be evaluating me on, like a checklist?"

I wave a hand dismissively. "I have that list on my smartphone. I'll fill it out tonight. After we see how this goes."

"How long is that list?"

I stare up at the ceiling, pretending I'm deep in thought. "I'd say it's about five or six pages."

"You're a woman after my own heart."

"Do you have a long checklist?"

"I do, and it's incredibly long." He takes a beat, his baby blues strolling up and down my body. "Lots of things are incredibly long."

"Who's forward now?" I ask, acting all aghast, but I'm not aghast at all. I like long things.

"What can I say? It seemed apropos. By the way, I'm not imported. I was actually locally grown."

"Ah, so you're a farm-to-date man?"

"Yes, I was homegrown within a fifty-mile radius. Raised in Westchester. So you're really able to tick a ton of boxes tonight. Presuming farm-to-date is on that *long* checklist."

"I'm adding it now and checking it off," I say, and inside I am punching the sky.

This is the best date ever.

As the pink glow from the neon light installation flickers behind him, I decide to opt for more honesty since it seems to be working so far—and way better than sabotage, it turns out. "I probably shouldn't say this, but dating can seriously suck, and in the first ten minutes, you're more fun than anyone I've gone out with in a long time, and on top of that, you're an insanely handsome guy." I park my hands on my hips, narrowing my eyes. "What's wrong with you?"

He heaves a sigh. "Fine. I'll admit it. I'm terrible at following IKEA directions for putting furniture together. I know, you just follow the steps. But it's hard, and I am bad at it. Can you live with that?"

I frown, scrub a hand across my chin. "If I have to."

He steps closer, his eyes taking a tour again. "Also, you beat me to it. You're beautiful. But honestly, even if you were average looking, that would be fine too, because looks aren't the most important thing, and these first few minutes are my favorite too. In a long time."

Holy shit. He's a breath of rarified air. I'm smiling, he's grinning, his eyes are sparkling, and my insides are shimmy shimmy bang banging. "I agree. Looks aren't all that."

"So we're good, then? If you bore me, I'm gonna be out of here in like a half hour."

"That long? I'd have thought sooner. But I'm glad that the challenge is on, and it goes both ways. You better keep up with me, Herb Smith."

"Oh, I intend to. I absolutely intend to keep up with you."

We wander around the gallery, checking out the bizarre installations made of neon lights, and as we go, my skin warms, my heart squeezes, and my hope skyrockets. I like this guy, I like his ease of conversation. I like the way he snaps, crackles, and pops when he talks.

I bet there's something wrong with him though.

Except I can't go looking.

I need to maintain the anti-self-sabotage shield.

We stop in front of a bright yellow pair of neon lights that look like a balloon animal at certain angles. "Also, can we get one thing out of the way real quick?" he asks.

I slice a hand in the air. "There's not going to be any sex tonight."

Laughter seems to burst from him. "That's not what I was going to say, but it's good to know your ground rules. Just so we're clear, are all types of sex off the table?"

Twin spots of pink form on my cheeks. "Probably."

He steps closer, and I can smell him—his aftershave is woodsy and intoxicating. "What about kissing, can we kiss? Let's say that I meet some of the marks on your checklist, do you want to have a kiss at the end?" he asks, and I'm nearly drunk on him already.

I want a kiss right the hell now. "That seems reasonable," I say a little breathy. Then my mind trips back to his comment. "What did you want to get out of the way, then?"

He takes a deep breath. "Yes, Herb is my real name."

"I didn't think it was a fake name."

"Who would pick that as a fake name, unless you were trying to scare somebody off?"

"Your name doesn't scare me," I say, because I'm 100 percent unperturbed by his old-school name.

"Are you sure?"

I point to the light sculpture on the white wall. "I'm still standing here under this weird, bizarre, twisty-turny collage of rainbow neon lights. I'm sure."

He glances up at the art installation in question. "Isn't that the coolest thing?"

"It's so weird, it's like the perfect weird piece of art. I want to hang that in my apartment and have people come over and say, 'What is that?' And I'll reply with 'my innermost thoughts,'" I say, all haughty.

"You're devilish," he says in admiration.

"Perhaps I am."

I stare at him, amazed that it's already going this well. "By the way, why did you mention your name?"

His tone is softer, more direct. "I guess because I'm surprised you didn't. Most dates bring up my name, since it's unusual. They want to know if it's a nickname, if it's real, if it's a family name that my mom *had* to give me. Or a mistake."

"A mistake? Why would someone think it's a mistake?"

He shoots me a steely glare. "Herb? Let's cut to the chase. It ain't Chase. It isn't Hunter or Bennett or Foxface, or whatever cool names dudes have these days."

A smile crosses my lips, warming me from the inside out. "I don't give a foxface if your name is cool or uncool. But is there a story behind it?"

He chuckles in a self-deprecating way that's thoroughly endearing. "Herb was my granddad's name. It was supposed to be my middle name. But he passed away a few days before I was born, and well, my sentimental parents made it my first name."

"Aww. That's touching. A very sweet story."

"I'm stuck with it, but he was a great man, so it's all good. And I have the world's simplest last name, so go figure."

"I like both of your names. The juxtaposition of the old-fashioned next to the familiar is a refreshing combo. It makes you even more unique, like this date."

"Normally on dates I count the seconds until it's going to be over."

"Ouch. The seconds, really? Is it usually that bad that you have to count the actual seconds?"

He nods vigorously. "It's usually that bad."

"What's the shortest date you've ever been on?" I query as we stroll through another hall of the art gallery.

"I would say about twelve minutes and fifty-two seconds. We had nothing to say to each other, and it was evident when she wanted to talk about how to do her nails, then she showed me an Instagram video of how to do nails, and there was like sponges and glue, and it was Instagram. Have I mentioned it was Instagram?"

"I'm going to go out on a limb and admit it. I do not get the fascination with every single life hack for every single thing, for every type of makeup or every type of possible decoration you could put on your body or face, but it seems like everyone in a certain age range wants to do everything they've learned from Instagram."

He smiles. "Is it too early to say this is the best date I've been on in a long time?"

My grin matches his. "I don't think it's too early at all, but I think we really should reserve judgment until we finish the main attraction."

"Are you ready for it?"

"I'm so ready."

We finish the appetizer portion of our date and head over to devour the main course.

4

HERB

As we walk to the warehouse, we talk.

"Ever been to an escape room before?" We turn down a lively block in Tribeca.

She wiggles her eyebrows. "That sounds like a come-on."

"Maybe it is." I dive into an exaggerated seductive voice. "Want to come see my . . . escape room, baby?"

She purses her lips then drags a hand down her chest. "Oooh, yes. Show it to me now."

I growl, keeping up the routine, loving how easily I'm clicking with this woman. "Level with me. Are you an escape room virgin?"

She drops a demure expression on her face. "I am indeed."

"Me too," I say, returning to my normal voice. "But Evie thinks it's perfect for us since I love puzzles and you presumably do too."

"Crazy for them," she says, emphasizing the words with passion. "My job is kind of like a puzzle. Being an ethical hacker. You have to get into everything backwards." Then she talks more about some of the work she does, and it's fascinating. She practices hacking into security for banks, then giving them advice on where they have holes. "And it's sort of similar to what you do," she says. "Which is a puzzle too."

Instantly I know what she means.

"Since my patients can't talk?"

She smiles and nods. "Yes, that does make it quite a puzzle. It's like you need a whole other language."

We chat more as we weave through the moonlit streets in lower Manhattan, and as we do, I take a moment to admire her. I was being honest when I said if she wasn't pretty, it wouldn't matter.

And I meant it. To me, this kind of chemistry—instant and electric—matters so much more.

But I still find it kind of hard to believe she's as gorgeous as she is, and as interesting as she is. Clearly, something has to go wrong, like it did with Sandy.

I tense momentarily, picturing my ex.

Seeing her face.

Feeling the gut punch of her news that she was leaving on a jet plane.

But I don't want Sandy to infect this night.

I hoist those thoughts right out of my mind.

We stop at a light, and I put a hand on Olivia's arm then run my palm down her skin. "I hope I'm not being too forward by touching your arm."

She gazes at me. "You can definitely touch my arm. In fact, I hope I'm not being too forward by saying it gave me the shivers."

"Good shivers?" I ask as a cab screams by.

"Definitely the good kind."

"I can work with good shivers."

The light changes and we cross. "Good shivers are another item on the checklist," she says.

I mime checking it off.

She flashes a smile that ignites me, and I wonder why I took so long to say yes to Evie. But then the last time I felt this way was Sandy and—

Nope. Not going to do it. Not going to let her ruin the best night in ages.

No. *Years.*

Just focus on tonight.

When we arrive at the warehouse, the gamemaster opens the door and lets us inside, his tone that of a clandestine fellow from decades ago. "Hello, my secret agents. Welcome to the 1940s. We have your escape room ready for you."

The gamemaster ushers us down to a basement room, tells us our fellow agents were wrongly taken into police custody, and if we can find the clues and crack the case, we can set them free.

The clock is ticking.

I turn to Olivia. "Do you agree it would be completely embarrassing if we don't find our way out of here? After we both talked about our skill with puzzles?"

"Failure is not an option," she says, her tone intense.

Quickly and methodically, we survey the room. There are wigs, trench coats, mustaches, and maps of the world that look like they belong in an old-time professor's office. A framed portrait hangs behind a large oak desk with a green lamp.

The portrait features a stern-looking man. "His left eye is wonky," I say, pointing to the picture and the way the eye seems askew.

She peers more closely. "It sure is."

She spins around, counting quietly. "And there are nine mirrors in this room."

I catalog the reflective surfaces—mirrors hanging on walls, one standing on a desk, another next to a globe.

"Mirrors and a wonky eye," I say, tapping my skull.

We spend the next thirty minutes with a laser focus, gathering clues, solving riddles, and cracking codes. We're nearly there. I can feel it. We stand at the desk, poring over one of the last clues, tossing ideas back and forth.

"This is so cool," she says. "If we're good at this, can we make it a thing?"

I laugh, loving that she's already decided we're having another date. "We can definitely make it a thing. We'll tackle all the escape rooms in New York City. How many do you think there are?"

"Thousands," she says softly, tilting her face toward me.

I hold her gaze, not wanting to look anywhere else but into her sparkling blue eyes.

"Olivia," I say, stepping closer to her, a rush of warmth skating over my skin, "are you telling me one hour into this date that you're having such a good time you want to go on a second date?" I don't know why I'm being so forward, yet I know exactly why I'm being so forward. Because she's fascinating. She's interesting. I've never felt this kind of instant, quick, sharp, spicy, tangible connection with somebody. Rather than run away from it, I don't want to let it go.

A lock of her hair is out of place, so I brush it off her shoulder. Her breath seems to hitch. "Yes. I do want to go on another date."

Somewhere in the back of my mind, I'm vaguely aware of a ticking clock. But I want this more. I run the back of my fingers across her cheek. "Is kissing on your checklist?"

She gasps softly. "I would say kissing *you* is on my checklist, but you have to be a really good kisser to stay on my checklist."

I move my hand to her face, sliding my thumb along her jawline. "It's on mine too."

"Let's check it off." Her eyes flutter shut.

I lean closer to her and brush my lips over hers. I feel a whisper of breath that seems to ghost across her lips, and then the slightest gasp.

She trembles. I'm not even holding her or touching her, I'm just kissing her lightly, softly. And she's shuddering.

It's beautiful and too good to be true.

But it's all true, and it's happening.

I want to know what else makes her feel this way.

I want to be the one to make her feel this way.

The intensity of those twin thoughts shocks me, maybe even scares me a bit, given my past experience.

But everything feels so right about tonight.

And I know that we could easily spend the whole night in here kissing, but I also suspect she'll be ticked if we don't get out of here before the clock.

I separate.

She blinks. "Wow, now my head is foggy. I don't know if I can concentrate."

"I don't know if I can either. But you know what I like more than kissing you?"

"I can't believe there's anything you like more than kissing me," she pouts.

I loop a hand around her hip, my thumb stroking against her. "I like getting to know you."

She practically purrs. "Herb, let's get the hell out of here, go to a diner, and get to know each other more."

We work, solving the final clue when we position all the mirrors in the room so that they're shining into the portrait's eye. As soon as they do, his eye works like a laser, then opens the door to the escape room.

We laugh and tumble out of the warehouse. The gamemaster tells us that was one of the fastest times that two people have actually executed an escape.

"Guess we had something we wanted outside of the room," I say, glancing at Olivia, who smiles back at me. We want to keep getting to know each other.

I thank the man and turn down the street, reaching for her hand.

She links her fingers through mine.

And am I ever glad I'm moving beyond the past.

Maybe this is insta-like. Heck, maybe it's insta-fall-ing. But screw it. I'm feeling it everywhere.

We wind up at a nearby diner ordering burgers,

French fries, and iced tea, and talking. We both agree Madison Square Park is our favorite park in the city, declaring the bench near the MetLife Building a great spot for kissing, then I tell her I like rock, and while she prefers pop, we agree we can coexist on the music front, since everything else is in sync. We chat until we close the place down.

At the end, it feels like we've been on three dates.

"Does this kind of feel like we've already hit the trifecta of three great dates?" I ask.

"It kind of does."

"And each one has been better than the last."

"They're all so good . . . it's almost as if it's too good to be true," she says, her tone light and breezy.

I stop, tug on her hand, and pull her flush against me. "But it's real." My voice is serious.

"It is?" Her tone is pocked with nerves. She looks unsure.

I nod, then cup her cheek and kiss her lips once more, savoring her taste, learning the flavor of her kiss, taking mental snapshots of how she feels in my arms.

Like she's giving herself to me.

And it's entirely what I want.

One freaking date, and I'm sold.

"It's not too good to be true," I say as we break apart, and I walk her home. But along the way, something seems to shift in her.

Her stance is stiffer. Her eyes are cooler. Her tone reads distant.

When we reach her place, I squeeze her hand. "You okay?"

"I'm great, but I'm so tired, and I need to go. Bye."

She spins around, heads up her steps, and darts inside without a parting glance.

I stand on the street wondering what the hell went wrong.

5

OLIVIA

Misery is my companion.

It trips me up on the racquetball court the next morning.

With an unladylike grunt, I lunge for the ball, and I smack it wildly. It screams across the court, missing the mark by miles.

Flynn thrusts his arms in victory.

I'm not annoyed he won. I'm simply annoyed. With myself. My thoughts are only on Herb Smith, and how badly I botched last night.

"Rematch?" Flynn asks, eagerness in his eyes.

I don't have the energy to attempt to even the score with my brother. "Nah."

He sets down his racket on the bench. "Clearly something is horribly wrong. Confession time." He pats the wood. "Tell me how you messed up last night."

I can't pretend I didn't. Misery slithers down my spine. "We were having the world's most perfect date," I say, forlorn.

"Yeah, yeah, skip over the sex part."

"We didn't have sex."

"Okay, you didn't have sex, so how could it have been the world's most perfect date?"

I swat him with my towel. "Things do not have to have sex to be awesome."

"But sex does help to make things awesome."

"You know how you didn't want to talk about how I look good in clothes? I don't want to talk about sex with you."

"Okay, fine, so you're having an awesome date." He makes a rolling gesture for me to keep going.

"We hit it off, Flynn. We had insane chemistry. We talked about everything, including how much we liked each other already. That's what freaked me out. We liked each other from the beginning."

His brow knits. "So you're worried it's insta-love?"

"But I don't believe in insta-love."

"Except you felt insta-love for him?" he points out gently.

My stomach flips with the sweetest memories of Herb's kisses, his words, his easy way with me. "I did. That's the thing. I felt insta everything for him." I toss up my hands and look to my brother. "Clearly, there's no way that can work. It's impossible, so I took off at the end."

"That's real mature," he deadpans.

"I couldn't fathom that it was all real . . . And then, what if I'd invited him up?"

"Let's play this game," Flynn says, thoughtful and logical. "What would have happened? What were you so scared of? Having real feelings for someone you truly like?"

A movie reel plays before my eyes. "I would have had hot, dirty sex with him, and I would have said, 'Let's get married and make babies,' and he'd have said yes, and it would be too good to be true."

"Wait. I thought we weren't supposed to talk about sex. You just said you had hot and dirty sex."

"In my dreams. Yes, it was going to be the hottest sex of my life because I'm that attracted to him. He kissed me in the middle of an escape room, and it was incredible. My toes are still tingling from it."

"Why are you standing here with me, then?"

"I don't know. That's a good question." I swallow hard, my throat burning.

He sighs, shaking his head. "Olivia, you're doing it again."

I sigh. I don't fight the truth this time. "I know. I'm sabotaging it. Because I'm afraid."

"And you like this guy. So, woman up and un-sabotage it."

6

HERB

The morning brings no more answers.

Only a gigantic question mark when I check my phone and find zero messages from her.

Then again, I didn't text her either.

I don't need to have her reject me again. Doing it to my face last night was all I needed, thank you very much.

Still, the clinical part of me wants to understand what went down.

As the sun rises, I dribble a basketball on the court in Central Park then send it soaring into the net.

"And then she just left," I tell my buddy Malone, a fellow vet.

"She sounds crazy."

That's Malone for you. He tends to think most people have lost a few, or several, marbles. He grabs the ball and whooshes it toward the net.

I grab it on the rebound. "It was literally the definition of a perfect date. Then she said, 'I'm so tired, and I need to go.'"

"Ouch. Sounds like she didn't want to see your sorry ass naked."

I roll my eyes. "My ass is spectacular, clothed or naked."

He shudders, like he's watching a horror flick. "Don't tell me anything more about your ass."

"I'm just saying, it's a gold-standard ass. She was checking it out."

He covers his ears. "Stop. Make it stop."

I shoot the ball, watching it arc into the net. "Anyway, that's that. She made it clear. There's nothing more that's going to happen. So I'll just move on."

He grabs the ball, stops, and stares at me. "Wait. That's your takeaway?"

"Well, what should it be?"

"You like this woman, you had a great date, she got wiggy at the end, and you're all *walk away*?"

"You said she was crazy."

He taps his chest. "Don't listen to me, dude."

"Who should I listen to?" I'm thoroughly perplexed.

"You like her, you had chemistry, and you had one weird moment. Dating is weird. It's like when you put a sweater on a cat and they don't know how to walk."

I furrow my brow. "Pretty sure Olivia knows how to walk."

Malone hums. "But you might need to help her take off the sweater."

"Man, your analogy game needs work. Are you saying I need to undress her?"

"No." His eyes bug out. "I'm saying you need to try again with her."

I crack up, clapping him on the back. "Wow. I didn't get that at all from the cat sweater analogy."

"Just try. The worst that'll happen is you're back out there on the dating circuit, putting sweaters on cats."

Maybe, just maybe, he's right. Maybe I should try to decipher what happened, because that really was the perfect date. And I don't want to give up this time.

7

OLIVIA

Later that day, I track down my matchmaker. We have lunch, and I tell her what happened.

"I really messed up."

Evie pats my hand. "No, sweetie, you didn't mess up, you got nervous. People get nervous. That's what happens. The question is—where do you go now?"

"I want to see him again. I think he's the one."

She beams. "I believe that too. But you're going to have to make it clear you're not a runner. That you're a stayer. Because I'm pretty sure he wants you to stay."

"Does he?" Tingles sweep through my body.

"The two of you are meant to be."

I quirk an eyebrow. "Do you believe in that? That people are meant to be together?"

"I do. Now you need to do what you should have done last night."

And I don't wait. I whip out my phone at lunch, dial his clinic, and ask to speak to Dr. Smith.

Evie beams the whole time, the proud matchmaker.

"He's with a patient right now. May I take a message?" The man on the other end of the phone asks.

With a smile, and a belly full of nerves, I give him a message. "Can you please tell Dr. Smith that it's Olivia and I would like to know if he would want to work on my checklist at Madison Square Park tonight?"

"I'll give him the message."

Evie claps.

I set down my phone, catching a glimpse of a message icon in the status bar. With butterflies fluttering, I click it open. It arrived fifteen minutes ago.

Herb: Hey, Olivia, so I'm not really sure what went wrong last night, but I'd like to try again with you. If you're up for it, maybe we can meet at Madison Square Park after work.

He must have sent it before I even called him. Oh God, I think I'm falling in love. My fingers speed through the fastest reply in the world.

Olivia: YES!!!!!! I'm there!

* * *

We arrive at the same time.

He walks toward me. I walk toward him. I stop in front of the bench, nerves and hope clogging my throat.

"I'm sorry I freaked out last night."

He sits and I sit next to him. "Are you a runner? Because once I have you as mine, I'm not going to want you to run away."

I take a deep breath. "I had a bad relationship. He cheated on me with a ton of other people, and sometimes I sabotage dates when it seems like it might work. I especially do when it's too good to be true."

He smiles and runs his thumb over my jawline. "So you think I'm too good to be true?"

"You said it yourself last night. Everything seemed that way."

"And that scared you?"

"It did. But that's no excuse." I reach for his hand. When he threads his fingers through mine, I swear all is right in the world. "Maybe it's too soon. Maybe it's too much. But I want to know what we can be."

He sighs, but it sounds like it's full of happy relief. "Look, I was hurt too. I was in love with this woman, and she took off around the world. I keep waiting for someone to pull the rug out from under me again."

My heart aches for him. "I don't want to pull the rug out from under you."

He sweeps his thumb over my jaw. "And I don't want to hurt you. All I want is to make you feel good."

And my heart—it soars to the sky. "That's the past. This is the present." I smile, and the way he smiles back at me, all crooked and sexy, sends heat through my body.

"There's only one way to find out if this thing is too good to be true," he says, his voice low, husky. His hand slinks around my neck, into my hair, sending shivers down my spine.

"To do this thing."

"Let's do this thing." He dips his face to my neck then kisses me there. "You know what escape room I'd like to go to right now?"

"Which one?" I'm trembling with desire.

"There's one in my apartment."

I moan. "If you take me there, I'm not going to want to escape."

"That's the plan."

I plant a kiss on his lips, and it's better than last night. It's wonderful and magical, and I feel it everywhere. Everything else fades away but the absolute magic of this man and me. Maybe I'm crazy, but I swear I can taste forever in his kiss.

I make a choice.

To break my habits and make brand new ones.

Starting with the hot, dirty sex I'd hoped for.

It's spectacular.

I suppose that's how it goes when you've finally met the man who ticks all the boxes and then some.

* * *

Herb

. . .

The next morning I take her out for pancakes.

With her fork in hand, she dives in with gusto. "I love pancakes."

"It's hard not to love pancakes."

"Hey! Don't rain on my pancake parade." She eyes my plate of eggs. "Why didn't you order pancakes?"

I sigh heavily and level with her. "I don't like them."

Her blue eyes pop. "What? How is that possible?"

"Just don't. I'm an eggs and hash browns kind of guy."

She shakes her head vehemently. "I refuse to believe anyone can dislike pancakes."

I tap my chest. "This guy does."

She huffs, takes another bite of her pancakes, then smiles. "Herb." She sets down her fork and gives me a strange smile.

"What? Is this a dealbreaker? A new act of sabotage?"

She stands, moves around the table, and sits down next to me, then kisses my cheek. "You told me you hate pancakes, and I still like you. This must be the real thing."

I laugh, cup her cheek, and bring her close for another kiss.

"And amazingly, I can tolerate the taste of pancakes on your lips."

She tap-dances her fingers down my shirt. "I'll get you to like them eventually."

"We'll see about that."

I walk her home, and outside her apartment she

gives me the best redo ever—kissing the hell out of me and making me wish I could take the rest of the day off.

Instead, I peel myself away, send her a text, and ask if I can see her that night.

Seconds later, she replies with a yes.

EPILOGUE

Olivia

I spend the night. And the next night, and the next one, and the next one.

For several wonderful blissful months that culminate in a ring, a promise, and a shared home.

Right now, I'm heading to meet Evie to thank her for setting me up with the man who has become my fiancé. When I see her at the coffee shop, Flynn is with her. "If we could only convince Flynn to let me work on him," Evie says, crossing her fingers.

He shakes his head. "Nope. I'm too focused on work."

I shoot him a *you're so ridiculous* look, then turn to Evie. "Someday he'll realize there is a meant-to-be for him, since I found mine. And we're going to Bora Bora for our honeymoon."

Flynn's green eyes light up. "He passed the Bora Bora litmus test."

"And someday you'll find someone who passes yours," I say.

My brother might be reluctant, he might have his own reasons for keeping up his guard, but I believe that deep down, there's a woman who's going to be his perfect match.

I found mine.

I thought he was too good to be true.

Then I realized that some things simply are, and those are the ones you don't let slip away.

THE END

Intrigued by Flynn? He has his own story to tell in COME AS YOU ARE, the smash hit romance that'll have you swooning, out now!

ALSO BY LAUREN BLAKELY

FULL PACKAGE, the #1 New York Times Bestselling
romantic comedy!

BIG ROCK, the hit New York Times Bestselling standalone
romantic comedy!

MISTER O, also a New York Times Bestselling standalone
romantic comedy!

WELL HUNG, a New York Times Bestselling standalone
romantic comedy!

JOY RIDE, a USA Today Bestselling standalone romantic
comedy!

HARD WOOD, a USA Today Bestselling standalone
romantic comedy!

THE SEXY ONE, a New York Times Bestselling bestselling
standalone romance!

THE HOT ONE, a USA Today Bestselling bestselling
standalone romance!

THE KNOCKED UP PLAN, a multi-week USA Today and
Amazon Charts Bestselling bestselling standalone romance!

MOST VALUABLE PLAYBOY, a sexy multi-week USA Today Bestselling sports romance! And its companion sports romance, MOST LIKELY TO SCORE!

THE V CARD, a USA Today Bestselling sinfully sexy romantic comedy!

WANDERLUST, a USA Today Bestselling contemporary romance!

COME AS YOU ARE, a Wall Street Journal and multi-week USA Today Bestselling contemporary romance!

PART-TIME LOVER, a multi-week USA Today Bestselling contemporary romance!

UNBREAK MY HEART, an emotional second chance USA Today Bestselling contemporary romance!

BEST LAID PLANS, a sexy friends-to-lovers USA Today Bestselling romance!

The Heartbreakers! The USA Today and WSJ Bestselling rock star series of standalone!

The New York Times and USA Today

Bestselling Seductive Nights series including

Night After Night, *After This Night*,

and *One More Night*

And the two standalone

romance novels in the Joy Delivered Duet, *Nights With Him* and Forbidden Nights, both New York Times and USA Today Bestsellers!

Sweet Sinful Nights, Sinful Desire, Sinful Longing and Sinful Love, the complete New York Times Bestselling high-heat romantic suspense series that spins off from Seductive Nights!

Playing With Her Heart, a

USA Today bestseller, and a sexy Seductive Nights spin-off standalone! (Davis and Jill's romance)

21 Stolen Kisses, the USA Today Bestselling forbidden new adult romance!

Caught Up In Us, a New York Times and

USA Today Bestseller! (Kat and Bryan's romance!)

Pretending He's Mine, a Barnes & Noble and

iBooks Bestseller! (Reeve & Sutton's romance)

My USA Today bestselling

No Regrets series that includes

The Thrill of It

(Meet Harley and Trey)

and its sequel

Every Second With You

My New York Times and USA Today

Bestselling Fighting Fire series that includes

Burn For Me

(Smith and Jamie's romance!)

Melt for Him

(Megan and Becker's romance!)

and *Consumed by You*

(Travis and Cara's romance!)

The Sapphire Affair series...

The Sapphire Affair

The Sapphire Heist

Out of Bounds

A New York Times Bestselling sexy sports romance

The Only One

A second chance love story!

Stud Finder

A sexy, flirty romance!

CONTACT

I love hearing from readers! You can find me on Twitter at LaurenBlakely3, Instagram at LaurenBlakelyBooks, Facebook at LaurenBlakelyBooks, or online at LaurenBlakely.com. You can also email me at laurenblakelybooks@gmail.com

Printed in Great Britain
by Amazon